MW00884025

SUMMER'S DESIRE

COWBOY SEASONS BOOK ONE

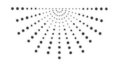

KATHLEEN BALL

Copyright © 2018 by Kathleen Ball

All rights reserved.

No part of this book may be reproduced in any form or by any electronic or mechanical means, including information storage and retrieval systems, without written permission from the author, except for the use of brief quotations in a book review.

❀ Created with Vellum

I dedicate Summer's Desire to my dad, James Tighe. I love you, Dad.

A special dedication to my amazing cousin Molly Garvin Doherty, a very talented author.

I want to thank Carih Haefs, Jean Joachim, JP Grider, Amber Dane, Stefan Ellery, My editor Rebecca Hollada, Lindsay Downs, Liberty Ann Ireland, all my Marine Moms, and Sandy Sullivan.

I especially I want to thank you for reading my books.

And to my loves, Bruce, Steven and Colt and Clara, because I love them.

CHAPTER ONE

Summer Fitzgerald eyed each shirtless cowboy before her. Something wasn't right. She was supposed to be the nanny/housekeeper for these young men? She answered the ad assuming she'd be mothering young boys.

Hell, these boys outgrew toys a long time ago. The oldest appeared to be about eighteen and the rest looked only a little younger. They were probably only each a year apart. "Where are the rest?"

"You're looking at all of us," said the second tallest.

The oldest elbowed the one beside him. "Put your shirts on. I heard it isn't polite to be without a shirt in front of a lady."

"I'm Matt—this here yahoo is Mark, Luke is next and the little squirt is John."

Her eyes widened. They intended to grow bigger? "Nice to meet you, I'm Summer. But I have a feeling I'm in the wrong place. I answered an ad to help out with boys."

John smiled. They all looked similar, brown wavy hair and deep brown eyes. "That's us, Ma'am."

"Surely you're old enough to take care of yourselves."

All the boys suddenly peered over her shoulder. Summer turned to see what they were looking at and almost gasped. Now this was a mature cowboy, an extremely handsome one at that. He would be the oldest brother, older than her twenty-five years.

"Ma'am, I'm Holden O'Leary. I placed the ad. I need some help with these young whelps. I'm always working and I thought a woman might be needed around here to help out."

It was hard to pull her eyes away from Holden. His dark eyes entranced her. "I'm Summer. But I don't know about this. I was expecting little boys, not practically grown men."

"Can you cook?" Mark interrupted.

"Please stay. Give us a chance." The plea in Holden's voice tugged at her heart.

She stared at the ground and shuffled her feet. Would she be able to do the job? She glanced up at Holden and her heart raced. She shook her head. "I thought the job was for a live in nanny/housekeeper. Small children I can handle but I'm not sure about teenagers. It wouldn't be a good fit for me."

Holden took a step toward her. His wide shoulders were broader up close. "I apologize. I know I stretched the truth a bit."

"Stretched? You totally misled me, and I don't know if I can work for someone who isn't up front with me."

His grin was a mix of guilty and sexy. "Look, I'm really sorry. Damn. We're not off to a good start are we? I'd be obliged if you'd reconsider. The last two are really just babes."

Luke, a smaller version of his eldest brother, stepped forward with a wide scowl on his face. "Babes? I'll show you a babe." He lowered his head and lurched forward, butting his head into Holden's abdomen.

Holden grabbed Luke by the collar of his shirt. "What do

you think..." Holden glanced her way and smiled, letting Luke go. "We don't usually fight."

Laughter started to bubble up inside her and she quickly suppressed it. Holden wasn't telling her the truth about anything as far as she could tell.

Taking a deep breath, she surveyed her surroundings. The house appeared sound, and it was certainly big; a two story place with a wide front porch. The barn seemed well kept and the horses in the corral were prime. A flawless view of the mountains awed her. Whoever first settled this place had picked a perfect piece of land.

Any objections faded away as she remembered how much gas she didn't have in her car. It was barely enough to take her back to Carlston. But, she would come up with something. "Nice to meet y' all but I'll pass." She turned and walked to her car. She just opened the car door when a big, tan, hand grabbed it.

"I'll pay you double."

The offer made her hesitate and she turned around. Holden's dark eyes were wide, desperate. Letting go of the door she crossed her arms in front of her. "I haven't seen you around town. When I saw the ad, I assumed you were a new family that moved into the area." She stared at him. "With children."

"It's a long story but we are new to the area. We needed a new start and here we are. I'm a veterinarian and—"

"Say no more. I heard a new vet was coming to town. You are planning to work with Colt O'Malley and his rescue horses aren't you?" She held her breath. She'd know what type of man he was by his answer.

"Colt invited me up here. We plan to work very closely. I always wanted to get involved with animal rescue operations."

Summer breathed out slowly. She assessed him one more

time, and then nodded. "If Colt knows you then I'll stay. Just so you know up front, no funny business."

Holden frowned. "Funny business?"

"Y'all keep your hands to yourselves."

Holden laughed, his dark eyes crinkled in the corners. "You don't have to worry about that. I can promise you that we don't need or want that type of thing from you."

That was the answer she wanted but somehow she still felt insulted. "Well good. I'd like to see the house now."

"Matt, can you show Summer the house?"

Matt walked toward them, a smile on his face. His dark brown hair reached his shoulders and upon closer inspection, she saw his dark eyes had a hint of amber in them. He had the build of a young adult that was bound to grow bigger.

"This way, Ma'am."

HOLDEN WATCHED Summer walk toward the house. She had long, honey blonde hair that blew in the wind, and he could tell by her flashing blue eyes that she had a lot of spirit. Realizing that he was watching her rear end as she walked, he quickly glanced away. He meant what he said to Summer about no funny business. No women, except for cooking, cleaning and looking after the boys. Hell, he'd had to uproot them all and move from Texas to Montana because of his lousy judgment in women and he was not going to put his family at risk again.

"Do we get to keep her?" John asked, his expression hopeful.

"For the time being," Holden told him. "I need to get going. Lots of animals to see today. Stay out of trouble and make sure you work with the horses and get the rest of the chores done."

Mark, Luke and John all nodded and watched him leave. He hoped Summer was still there when he came back. His brothers could be a handful and truth be told, they were just boys. But if Summer didn't work out, he'd find another solution. He'd been finding another solution for years now. They'd be fine.

He drove into the small town of Carlston, passing Rex's Barber Shop, Ander's Food Mart, and Lucy's Deli. His office sat between the community center and a big white church with a huge steeple. The town was much smaller than he'd anticipated, but the gossip was bigger than he imagined. Any hope for privacy deflated the moment Beverly Rain, the town librarian, visited his office last week.

Talk about a busybody. She didn't own any animals; she just wanted to know everything about him. Holden felt lucky to have escaped with only telling her a few bare facts the first time he met her. He found out later that day, however, she considered herself the town matron and society leader. All he knew was that she wore too much perfume, dyed her hair a magenta color and was a royal pain in the ass.

He was determined to make a go of it here in Carlston. His brothers needed a fresh start after all the trouble in Texas. Maybe if he'd hired someone to look after them then, things would be different. It wasn't worth rehashing but he did it daily.

Walking into the clinic he smiled at Mindy Sue, his veterinarian tech. Actually, she did much more than vet techs usually did and he was grateful for it. She answered phones, did all the lab work, and handled owner's questions. If things worked out he was going to pay for her to go back to school.

"Good morning, Holden." Her bright smile was always welcome.

"Morning, Mindy Sue." He noticed that her hair was blonde this morning. She changed color and styles so often he began to wonder if she wore wigs. Her light brown eyes beamed kindness and confidence. She had some interesting ideas about nail polish too or whatever it was she put on her nails. Always a different pattern, but he wasn't about to ask anything the least bit personal. He didn't want to have to answer any of those questions himself.

"Colt O'Malley needs you sometime today. Guess he had to rescue another horse last night. A mare. He said it's the usual but needs you to come take a look."

Holden ran his fingers through his hair and sighed. "I guess I thought since the town was so small there would be less animal abuse. I don't know what I was thinking."

Mindy Sue nodded, got up and went to the coffee pot on the counter. She poured a cup and handed it to Holden. "Times are tough. The price of hay has gone up and plenty of people are losing their ranches and farms."

Holden took a sip of the coffee. "Thank God for people like Colt. At least the horses have a place to go."

"Have you met Stone McCoy or Jonas Barnes?" He shook his head. "Well, you will soon enough. They take in the over-load. If Colt doesn't have room for a horse, Jonas and Stone jump in. It's a shame that extra room is needed at all. Jonas takes the ones that look like they won't make it. He likes to make their last days happy."

"He doesn't—"

Mindy Sue's eyes grew wide. "No, he doesn't put them down himself. That's your job."

"As it should be. I'm going to head out there now." He started to walk to the door and turned back around. "Do you know Summer Fitzgerald?"

"Yes I do. She's lived here all her life. There was some

trouble and I heard she got kicked out of her apartment. Why?"

"She's working at my place."

Mindy Sue nodded. "Good. She's in good hands then." He opened his mouth to ask another question but Mindy Sue put her hand up in front of her. "Stop right there. The trouble was not her fault in my opinion and you know I hate gossip. Ask her yourself."

"Fair enough. Call if you need me." He walked out the door. On the way to his pick-up he spotted Beverly Rain hurrying toward him and he wanted to run in the opposite direction. That woman never had anything pleasant to say.

"Wait, Doctor. I have news for you."

Holden bit back a few curses. "Good morning, Mrs. Rain."

"Yes, well it's Miss. If you are going to the O'Malley place you'd better know what you're in for."

"What would that be?" He really didn't have the patience for her today.

She looked pleased with herself. "The horse was taken from Jacob Ash. He's one mean son of a gun. Please be warned. I wouldn't want anything to happen to the new doctor."

"Have a good morning." He bit back a smile. She did not like his dismissal at all, but the sour look on her face made his day. She opened her mouth and he walked away as fast as he could. Being friendly was one thing but gossip just plain hurt.

He hopped into his truck and wondered how things were going at home. Hopefully Summer was getting accustomed to the house and his brothers. They could be a handful and he didn't need her scared off the first day.

───────────

7

SUMMER PEERED around the big house and wanted to scream. It looked as though a storm had come through. There wasn't one empty, clean, spot in the whole place, with plates, cups, clothes, papers and mud spread throughout. No wonder Holden was so intent on having her stay.

She glanced at Matt. "Pigs live better."

"Now, Miss Summer, that's debatable with them living mostly outside and all." His lips twitched as though he was trying to contain laughter.

For a second she was tempted to wipe the grin off his face, but he was so darn cute. "Very funny. Now who usually cooks around here?"

It took him so long to answer she thought he hadn't heard her.

"Which day?"

Shaking her head she grinned. "I think I get the idea. No one cooks and no one cleans."

Matt shrugged his shoulders. "We do, when necessary." He shifted from one foot to the other staring at the mud caked floor.

She felt bad for him. Maybe he was really the shy type inside. "Go on to the horses and whatever else you men do. I will try my best to make a dent in this mess."

A smile swept his face as he glanced at her. "Start in the kitchen. I'm starved." He was out the door before she could answer him.

First, she'd have to clear a path to the kitchen. They hadn't unpacked from the move, so there were boxes everywhere. Holden said he'd pay her double, but now that she thought about it, she still had no idea how much the original pay was. A lapse of judgment on her part. She really didn't have anywhere to go, but if she didn't like it here she could wait until she got just enough money to put gas in her car and run for it. That was the big appeal of being a bartender.

You could find a job anywhere. Just not in Carlston, not anymore.

It'd been hazardous and time consuming moving boxes and making a clear path to the kitchen. It was not what she expected. The cabinets were polished maple, the stove and refrigerator were stainless steel. Summer chuckled and shook her head. She'd almost expected some kind of wood burning stove. It would be worth cleaning up here just to see what it all really looked like.

Hearing footsteps, she turned. The youth before her appeared just old enough to start shaving. He was well toned, probably from working the ranch. She tilted her head to look into his eyes. "You must be Mark."

He nodded as a shy smile crossed his face. "Is it true? Are you going to cook?"

Summer laughed. "If I can get this kitchen cleaned, that's the plan."

"Oh boy!" The excitement on his face warmed her.

"Mark, how old are you?"

"I'm sixteen, Ma'am." He stood a bit taller.

"How old is everyone else? And you don't have to call me Ma'am. Summer will do."

His smile was boyish and a bit lopsided. She liked him instantly. "Holden is twenty-six. Matt is eighteen, Luke is fourteen, and John is twelve."

"I see. I thought you all to be older."

"That's because we work as hard as any man and we're strong." His pride was unmistakable.

Summer nodded. "I believe you. Now I need to get back to the dishes, so you should get going unless you want to help."

His eyes widened in alarm. "No thank you, M—Summer. I have plenty to keep me busy."

He practically fled the house. They were just boys after

all, except for Holden of course. Maybe she could do some good here.

Long hours later, she finally glanced around the sparkling kitchen, proud of her hard work. The kitchen was absolutely beautiful. Everything from the floor to the faucets looked brand new, and during her deep clean she'd been lucky enough to find enough ingredients to make spaghetti and meatballs. Jarred sauce but it would have to do. There was even a biscuit mix she could use. Good thing she had a good teacher. The kitchen was her comfort zone. When she'd started as a bartender at The Carlston Bar and Grill, she didn't know much but the owner Paul had patiently taught her to cook and make a damn good martini.

Rest in peace Paul. A tear threatened to fall but she sucked it up.

"Done is done," her mother always said. There was no time to feel sorry for herself. She was still alive and able to kick where it counted.

The door opened and Holden walked in. She had a great view of him from the kitchen. Her stomach clenched and a shiver went up her spine. He was one fine specimen of maleness and her boss. This attraction needed to stop immediately. There was no sense admiring her boss when her focus needed to be those boys. She dried her hands with a clean towel, apparently the only one in the house.

"Wow." Holden's dark eyes reflected his appreciation. "You have been busy. This kitchen hasn't been this clean since we moved in." He made his way through the path she'd made in the great room. "I'm sorry the place is such a mess. I'm constantly on call and the boys…"

Summer smiled. It was nice to be appreciated for a change. "It's a beautiful kitchen. The Clarks owned this place, didn't they?"

Holden seemed caught up in admiring the kitchen. "Yes. I

guess the father is in a home and the son wanted to sell. He upgraded the whole house, but I would have taken it anyway. The land is prime."

"It is a beautiful view."

"Sure the view is great but I'm talking about ponds and streams and lush grass." He had a faraway look in his eyes as he stepped toward her.

His shoulders were wider than she thought and he was much taller. His hips were slim and his legs appeared solid under his Wranglers. She stepped away from him and walked to the other side of the kitchen, putting the large table between them. "You're right by the way. Your brothers are really boys."

"That's why I need someone. I can't be everywhere and you can see what a disaster I've made of the house. Truthfully, my practice has three times the patients than I was told."

"You call the animals the patients? What about the humans?"

"They are just the owners. Some should be hung out to dry." Sighing loudly, he sat down and ran his fingers through his thick hair.

"Bad day at the office?"

"Something like that. Colt had a mare named Yo-Yo he rescued. The poor thing's ribs and spine were showing. She has severe rain rot, dental problems and overgrown feet. Not good at all."

"How the hell does that happen?"

Holden gave her a sad smile. "Unfortunately it's not an isolated case. Happening a lot more these days. Do you know Colt O'Malley?"

"Sure, and his brother Caleb. Nice guys."

Holden nodded without taking his gaze off her. "Met him today, good man. I'm supposed to meet Stone

McCoy and Jonas Barnes tomorrow. They handle rescues too."

"I went to school with Jonas. He's a great guy. Stone moved here a few years ago. I don't know too much about him except he's a decent person and a good rancher. He asked me out on a date once."

"I take it you didn't go?"

"No, I'm leaving all the eligible bachelors for the rest of the women in town. I'm fine on my own."

His gaze grew piercing. "That explains it."

Her hands became sweaty and a lump formed in her throat. "Explains what?"

"I was wondering why you're single. You are, aren't you?"

Summer frowned. She didn't like personal questions and she didn't want him in the kitchen. "You do know that a woman doesn't need to get married don't you? We can support ourselves. Now I have to finish getting dinner ready."

Holden nodded and started to walk to the door. He stopped and stared at her. "Well?"

"Oh for heaven's sake. I'm single. No one would have me." She instantly wished she could take her outburst back. His eyes widened as he looked her up and down, and his assessing embarrassed her. Of course she'd had boyfriends but she somehow always found the jerks. It wasn't as though she was a raving beauty who attracted tons of guys.

Holden started to march back toward her.

"Get your brothers and tell them it's time to eat." She didn't want any false compliments.

He hesitated as though puzzled, but shrugged his shoulders and headed out the door.

HOLDEN TRIED NOT to laugh at his brothers. They'd never acted so polite and well-mannered before. All through dinner they said please and thank you and they complimented Summer's cooking constantly. It was damn good he had to admit.

He felt bad leaving to get the boys for dinner. Why would she say something as ridiculous as no one would have her? She was pretty enough and her figure was nice. If he was being honest it was better than nice. She seemed sane enough too. His face grew warm as he realized he'd been staring at her like some moon-eyed youngster. He glanced down at his plate instead. He didn't need anyone getting ideas of becoming involved with him.

"Right, Holden?" Luke kicked him under the table.

"Ow. What is wrong with you?" He was immediately sorry for his outburst when he saw Luke's frown. "Luke, what did you want?"

Luke's face turned red. He quickly glanced at Summer and just as quickly looked away. "I was just sayin' that she'd be hard put to find a place to sleep tonight."

Holden leaned over and ruffled Luke's hair. "You giving up your bed, bud?"

An impish grin crossed Luke's face. "Nah, I'm a boy, remember? I need my sleep. Now you being an old man and all…" Luke chuckled.

Luke's laugh was infectious and soon they were all laughing. Holden locked eyes with Summer. Her blue eyes were filled with mirth and it was nice to see her smile. "Guess I hadn't thought this whole thing out. Summer, you can have my bed."

"No, no that's okay," she protested. "The couch is fine."

"No, the couch isn't a good idea. I get calls all night to help animals. I don't want to worry about disturbing your sleep."

"If you're sure?"

Holden pushed back from the table and stood. "Guys, help me get this couch cleared off. Been so long I've forgotten what color it is."

The boys each left the table and grabbed things off the couch. Everything from socks to harnesses was cluttering it. Holden laughed and held up a pocket watch. "I've been looking all over for this."

Matt stopped and nudged him. "How about your room? Is it decent for a lady?"

Summer stepped toward them. "If you have clean sheets I can make the bed."

"Anyone know where the sheets are?" Holden asked hopefully. "Well, we'll have to look in a couple boxes and find them."

Mark laughed. "A couple boxes?" He nodded toward the stacks of unpacked boxes, dark eyes full of humor.

They all looked through boxes. Matt and Holden tackled the taller stacks while the others searched in the boxes they could reach, until Luke yelled, "Found them!"

Holden took them and turned to hand them to Summer, except she wasn't there. "Where'd she go?"

"Your room?" Mark suggested.

John shook his head. "We'd have heard a scream if she went in there. Holden is the biggest slob here."

Holden's jaw dropped open. "What's that supposed to mean?"

"It means that you need to get up here and help me," Summer called down.

Matt immediately headed for the stairs. Holden caught up to him and put his hand on Matt's shoulder. "My mess. I'll take care of it."

Matt scowled at him and his gut clenched. He hoped that Matt didn't have another crush on a woman too old for him.

Shaking his head, he climbed the stairs vowing to keep an eye on that one.

"He's right you know." Summer stripped the sheets off the bed.

"Who?"

"John. I almost did scream but I thought I'd save that for my second day on the job."

"I am not—" He stopped when he saw her grinning at him. "Alright I admit it. I'm not a neat freak."

"A neat freak? No, Holden, not even close." She laughed and the sound lightened his heart a bit..

"I'm sorry. I really didn't plan very well."

"Holden, I'm surprised that you even have time for a job. I can tell you love your brothers. That makes up for a lot."

He glimpsed pain in her eyes and wondered about it. He had his own personal problems that he didn't want to divulge, so he wouldn't ask about hers. "I'll help you make the bed."

She hesitated and he got the feeling she'd rather do it alone. "On second thought, why don't I just carry the laundry downstairs? I'll need to get a few things out of here for tomorrow and for tonight. My hours…well I sleep when I can."

"It's fine," Summer walked to the corner of the room furthest away from him, avoiding his gaze. In fact, she suddenly found the sheets fascinating and kept staring at them.

Grabbing the laundry, he glanced at her. Nothing. One minute she was laughing and the next, well, he didn't know what was going on.

He carried his laundry downstairs and found his brothers all watching some murder mystery on TV. The quiet was welcome. He walked back to his room for the rest and Summer stood in the same corner still staring at the sheets.

"Is there something wrong with the sheets?"

Her head popped up. "No. I was just waiting for you to get your things. I'm pretty tired."

"You're sure you don't want me to help make the bed?"

"No. I mean thank you but I can handle it." Grabbing the sheets, she finally began to make the bed.

"Summer?"

"Yes?"

He wanted to ask about her sudden change, but thought better of it. "Good night."

"Good night." She nodded and looked up, but not at him. She gazed just to the left of him.

Before he had any more time to try to puzzle her out, his phone rang. A man in the next county had tried to load up two trailers full of horses to be sold as horse meat. There were already two vets on the scene but Colt asked if he could come too.

"Damn, I have to go."

"You look worried." Summer's brow furrowed as she studied him.

"I need to rescue some horses. Look I know this is your first night and all and the boys—"

"We'll be fine. You go, you're needed and I'll take care of the boys. Don't worry, I can handle it." Her voice exuded confidence.

"Thanks." Rushing around he grabbed clean clothes to take downstairs. Before he left he gave her a long look, nodded and then flew down the stairs.

The boys barely glanced up when he explained he had an emergency to attend to. They were used to his schedule. They didn't even say goodbye as he left. Shrugging his shoulders he wondered if it was a good thing that he wouldn't be missed.

SUMMER SAT up in Holden's bed and stretched her arms over her head. It had been a night of constant interrupted sleep. She'd heard Holden leave and she fell asleep only to be woken later by a cry from one of the boys. Rushing out of her room, she found John shouting out in his sleep. She woke him and held him for a few minutes until he told her he was too old for mollycoddling. Returning to her room, she checked the couch, and still no Holden. She went back to bed but sleep came hard. Finally, she heard Holden come in around two o'clock. After that she drifted off.

Sometime around five in the morning, she pulled herself out of bed. She went to the bathroom first thing and grimaced, quickly noting that cleaning it would take priority today. Then she tip-toed down the stairs after she got dressed. The boys were bound to be hungry and if the amount they ate last night was any indication, she needed to cook a lot. But coffee first. Nothing sat well with her before coffee. The sun was just rising in its yellow, orange and red glory. The summer season was certainly here.

The house felt a bit warm but she didn't dare turn on the air conditioning. Who knew what the rules around here were? She made coffee and pulled the last of the eggs out of the refrigerator. Someone would have to go shopping. She really wasn't up to going into town if she could help it.

She should probably just tell Holden before someone else did. Who knew what version he would get? She'd grown up in Carlston and had never been in real trouble. Her folks were hard working and so was she. But somehow her reputation was shredded all in one night. One awful night. A shiver went through her as she thought about it.

"Cold?"

She needed to be more aware of her surroundings.

Somehow Holden had snuck behind her and startled her. She put on what she hoped was her poker face and turned. Sexy was the first word that came to mind. His hair was sticking up and he had a day's growth of stubble. Definitely sexy.

"No. In fact I was thinking it was a bit warm in here. It's supposed to get pretty hot today. Do you open the windows, use fans, air conditioning?"

"I'll set the air before I get dressed. You're up early."

"Not really. I lived on a ranch most of my life before my parents died. I'm used to the hours."

He tilted his head as though he was trying to figure her out. "You ride?"

"Probably better than you." She couldn't help the smile that graced her face. "When I wasn't in school, I was in the saddle. In fact I didn't even know how to cook until Paul, the owner at my old job, taught me."

"Where are your folks now?"

"They both drowned two years ago." She shrugged her shoulders, but in truth her heart broke every time she told someone.

"I'm sorry, Summer." His eyes reflected a kindness that had been scarce in her life lately.

"You didn't get much sleep. Why don't you go back to bed?"

Holden reached around her and poured himself a cup of coffee. "It's been eons since anyone cared about my sleep or lack thereof. I'll be fine. The boys and I need to work with the horses and I have a small herd of cattle I need to check on this morning."

They both leaned back against the counter, sipping coffee. Surprisingly, the silence was comfortable. "I have a bathroom or two to tackle today. I might as well get some laundry done too."

After a bit, he set his coffee cup on the counter. "I'll be

back in time for breakfast. I'll be in the barn if you need me." With a quick nod, he left.

She wished she had taken the opportunity to tell him. She had the feeling that calm moments were a fleeting thing here.

A half hour later, the sound of footsteps and good natured banter soon confirmed her feeling as four boys came piling head long into the kitchen. They saw her and each straightened. Matt finger-combed his hair.

"Morning," she sang out. "Just in time."

John's eyes grew wide as he eyed the table. "Oh boy, a real breakfast!"

Summer smiled. "What do you usually eat?"

"Toast. Usually we have toast. If we don't get up on time, then you just get bread." John told her solemnly.

Summer wanted to laugh at his dramatics. "That's just plain awful, the bread and water treatment. Just who is in charge around here?"

"That would be me." Holden closed the door behind him and winked at her.

She flushed and got busy putting the bacon, eggs and toast on the table.

"So, who here drinks coffee?" It surprised her when they all chimed in. "Luke, John, you drink coffee? How about some milk?" Luke's hard look made her realize that she said the wrong thing.

"Coffee. Black," Luke said, slow and loud while he gave her a hard stare.

Matt hit Luke's shoulder. "Have some manners."

Luke turned red and hit Matt back. "At least I don't have the hots for the woman."

Holden stepped between them. "Matt, no hitting. Luke, you apologize to both your brother and to Summer. She is not 'the woman.' She has a name."

Luke hesitated and Matt threw down his napkin and slammed the door closed as he left.

"She thinks I'm some kid. If I want coffee, I expect coffee. Who is she to be asking anyway?"

"Luke," the warning in Holden's voice was evident.

"You are far from perfect," Luke spouted before he high-tailed it out the door too.

Mark and John appeared shell shocked. They sat straight up in their chairs staring at each other.

Summer sighed. "I'm sorry. I made a mess of things." Part of her wanted to cry, but she knew better than to cry at work. Tears never solved anything.

Holden shook his head. "No darlin', you did nothing wrong. I'm sorry that Luke's anger was directed at you. We've all been a bit touchy since... well since the move. I'll talk to them and have them apologize. For now let's eat. I'm starved and this all looks amazing."

She put the coffee pot on the table. They could pour their own after that fiasco. Sitting, she peered at Mark and John. They appeared decidedly uncomfortable but ate anyway. "I hope you like it." She tried to smile but she knew she didn't succeed. With this many males there were bound to be some stepped on toes. Men thought women were touchy. Obviously they didn't realize the truth.

"This is really good," John said with a full mouth.

Holden had his mouth open, probably to admonish him, but Summer picked up a piece of toast, leaned over and put a corner of it in Holden's mouth. His eyes widened in surprise for a second before he took a bite and they all laughed. The tension in the room broke and he sent her a look of gratitude. It made her smile.

"Really, this is good and I appreciate it." Holden wiped the side of his mouth with his napkin. "I have to get to the office. Mark, tell Matt that I don't want him trying to ride Yukon just yet. That horse still needs some work. John, I need the western fence line checked." John opened his mouth. "Before you argue, I don't care who does what. I just want it done."

Both Mark and John nodded.

"I should be back in time for dinner. Summer, I'll call and let you know."

Summer nodded too. "I have more than enough to keep me busy. Have a good day." She got up and cleared the table. One by one the others left. It was just an adjustment, she hoped. They really were just boys.

CHAPTER TWO

$\mathcal{H}$olden parked his truck in front of the community center. It galled him to see Beverly Rain run out toward him. Didn't she have books to tend? How big was the library anyway? Obviously not big enough to keep her busy. He slowly got out of the truck, grabbed his black Stetson and smashed it on his head.

A warm breeze washed over him and he was suddenly glad he turned the air conditioning on for Summer. It was bound to get warmer.

He tried to pretend he didn't see Beverly but she started yahooing at him. Resigned, he rolled his eyes then turned her way and put on a smile. As she came closer he could see her face full of glee. It was a sure bet she had gossip to share and he wasn't in the mood.

"Good morning, Doctor." She put her hand to her heaving chest as though she had just run a marathon.

"Ma'am." He tipped his hat and started around her.

She reached out and grabbed his arm. "I need to talk to you."

He gazed down at his arm and then stared at her, hoping

his "don't mess with me" stare worked. It always worked on his brothers.

"Now, now." She patted his arm. "I've something important to tell you."

"Spit it out." He wanted to laugh at her attempt to seem affronted.

"I just heard about Summer Fitzgerald. You have been led astray and there is no way you can employ her. Why, what would the town think? It will kill your practice. She's real good with her innocent act but don't let her fool you. I'm telling you if the townspeople find out, they won't be happy."

Holden was sure if he didn't listen, she would go out of her way to tell each person what she thought.

"She was a bartender."

"I know. Nothing wrong with that."

"Did she tell you why she no longer works there?"

"No, and frankly it's none of my business." He hoped she'd get the message that he was not interested.

"Paul Gallagher owned the place and he treated her like a daughter."

"Listen, I really don't have time." He pulled his arm away and turned.

"Wait, I didn't tell you how she robbed the place."

Holden closed his eyes, wishing he never left the ranch. He had to hear her out now; he was responsible for his brothers. Turning back around, he stared at her again. She seemed flustered and he was glad.

"She planned the robbery with an old boyfriend, Brent. Paul was beaten to death and money was stolen. It's the most horrifying thing that has ever happened here."

"Why isn't she in jail?"

"Because she pretended to be a victim. She pretended that she was beaten unconscious. Her clothes were ripped but she wasn't violated."

"Violated?" He shouldn't have asked. Her smile became one of triumph.

"Yes, she wasn't raped and that is beyond fishy. I know she was desperate for money, but there just wasn't enough forensic evidence to charge her."

Forensics? Beverly Rain was no librarian, rather a watcher of crime shows. The glee in her eyes made his stomach turn. She seemed hell bent on causing trouble.

"I thank you, Mrs. Rain."

"It's Miss. I'm not married." She smiled at him.

Somehow she made him feel dirty in the moment. "Okay then, well you have a good day." He stalked to his clinic, barely said hello to Mindy Sue and stormed into his office.

He sat in his big leather chair shaking his head. Violated? If the gossip wasn't about Summer, he'd laugh. The whole thing was ridiculous, wasn't it?

A knock on his door pulled him from his musing. He'd been rude to Mindy Sue. "Come on in."

The door opened slowly and only Mindy Sue's head appeared. Her hair was platinum blonde today. "Is everything okay?"

Holden waved her in. "I'm sorry. How are you today, Mindy Sue?"

"I'm fine." She stared at him with one eyebrow arched.

He knew she was curious. "Any messages?"

"Only from Colt. He said to say thanks when you got in and that he hoped you didn't have to come in early."

Holden nodded.

Mindy Sue relaxed and smiled. "More horses needed rescuing?"

He ran his hand over his face, realizing he still had his Stetson on. He took it off, set it on his desk feeling weary. "A bunch of them were being transported to Canada for slaughter."

"I thought it was illegal now."

"Well that little technicality doesn't seem to discourage some people. I'm a bit cranky, so I'm going to do some paperwork and if the coast is clear, I might head on home early."

"It makes me so mad. Get your paperwork done and don't worry, I can hold down the fort."

"Thanks." He gave what he hoped was a grateful smile.

The door closed and he dived right into his work. He didn't want to think about what Beverly told him, but unfortunately his mind kept going back. Was there any truth to the story? Summer did say she had worked at the bar and grill and she mentioned an owner named Paul. When had all this taken place? She didn't look beat up to him.

Unable to concentrate on his work, he picked up his hat, smashed it back down on his head and headed out. He really wanted to hear Summer's side of the story.

He had his own past he didn't want anyone to know about. There were false allegations, but people believed the most salacious tidbits. It shocked him when people he'd known most of his life took sides against him. Matt was never charged and the truth came out but still everyone seemed glad when they left Texas.

No, he decided he wasn't going to ask her but he was going to keep an eye on her. If she had robbed the place why was she still in Carlston? Why bother to look for another job?

His brothers came first and he was determined they'd have fresh start. A little caution never hurt and if he balanced it with common sense laced with a dose of skepticism, things should be fine.

He made good time getting home and when he got there, all he wanted to do was sleep. He'd use one of his brother's beds. Hopefully he'd be able to think after a good rest.

Driving up, he spotted Summer hanging sheets on the line. They waved in the breeze billowing back and forth. Summer's honey blonde hair blew around her and she kept brushing it away from her face. It was hard to believe that she helped to rob and beat someone.

Caution, he reminded himself.

He walked up to the house without acknowledging her, hung his hat on the rack and headed upstairs. Glimpsing into Matt's bedroom he saw a naked mattress. There weren't any sheets on any of the other beds he checked either. All the beds were stripped. Groaning, he went back down the stairs to see if he could find any clean sheets.

As soon as his foot hit the bottom step, the front door opened. Summer entered appearing incredibly fresh and clean. Her blue eyes sparkled and she hummed a tune. Her humming stopped as soon as she spied him and the sparkle dimmed a bit.

"I didn't see you come in."

"My truck is outside."

She nodded. "So, are two others. I guess I didn't count them."

"I'm trying to find some sheets. I need some sleep."

Summer bit her bottom lip and shook her head. "They are all on the line. All but the ones I put on your bed. Take a nap in your own bed."

He'd been avoiding doing just that. The bed would have her scent and he needed rest, not dreams of her. "There's always the couch."

She put her hands on her hips and frowned. "Holden, how in the world do you expect to get any sleep? The boys are in and out all day and it'll just make things hard to do if I have to tiptoe around you."

Running his fingers through his hair, he tried to think of

another option. Nothing came to mind. "You're right. I'll get a few hours shut-eye."

Her smile made his heart flip over in his chest. It made him feel crazy. He didn't even know if she was trustworthy yet. His mind and body were warring and he didn't like it at all. He smiled back at her and she blushed, suddenly finding the floor more interesting than him. He quickly went back up the stairs. No more smiles and no more blushes. It was the quickest way toward trouble. Trouble he didn't need.

Lying in bed, he tossed and turned, sheets smelling like vanilla with maybe a hint of cinnamon. She smelled like a snickerdoodle except for a bit of musk. He hoped the other sheets dried quickly; he didn't get enough sleep as it was and he didn't need distractions. Hell, she was a distraction whether he wanted her to be or not and he found it hard to believe that little gal would be part of any crime. Damn, she hummed doing laundry and he just didn't know what to think. Just as he started to fall asleep, he decided that he needed to know what happened at the Bar and Grill.

SUMMER FOUND BREAD, deli meat and cheese and made a whole slew of sandwiches for lunch. Hopefully, Holden was getting his rest. Did he know he was beyond handsome? He didn't act as though he was aware of it but some woman must have told him before.

Mark raced in, his eyes wide and he was breathing hard. "Call a doctor!"

Alarm raced through her. "What happened?"

"Matt is hurt."

Summer felt the blood drain from her face. Hell, she was supposed to be watching them. "Go get Holden. I'll see to Matt." She didn't wait for a reply as she ran out the door.

Luke and John were inside the corral. Racing over, she spotted Matt on the ground. He seemed awfully still.

Before she even reached the boys, Holden raced by her, jumped the fence and knelt beside Matt. He examined every part of him without moving him while she prayed that it wasn't anything serious. Their faces were all anxious and John had tears in his eyes.

"Holden?" He didn't look at her. "Holden, is he going to be all right?"

"The ambulance is on the way." He nodded toward the bay horse on the other side of the corral. "Mark, I need you to secure Yukon."

Matt started to moan in pain. "Holden, it hurts. It hurts bad."

"I know, buddy. Yukon got the better of you. You have a busted ankle and a whole lot of bruises. I don't think your ribs are cracked but we'll see what the x-rays show."

"Holden, I'm sorry. I know I wasn't supposed to be on Yukon. Ouch, darn, ornery horse. Maybe you should just ship me off to school. Studying must be a nice safe thing to do."

Holden grabbed Matt's hand. "No. You are staying with us. We have fought long and hard to be together, to make a fresh start. Hell, it's just an ankle. Hardly a scratch."

Matt grinned then groaned. "No trick riding me for, I guess."

Holden patted Matt on the shoulder. "You never were good at that anyway. I wouldn't worry about it."

In amazement, she stared at the two brothers. How could they joke around? Her chest became tight, she found it hard to breathe and she had to clasp her hands together to keep them from shaking. Being a vet, Holden probably had to be calm in a crisis.

Finally, she heard the sirens and thanked God, when they

arrived. The expressions of fear on Mark, Luke and John's faces made her wince. This was her fault. It was her responsibility and the guilt gnawed at her.

The EMTs did an assessment of Matt, and then loaded him up into the ambulance. All the boys wanted to ride with him.

Holden stepped in front of her. His eyes said it all. He blamed her. "I'm going with Matt. Could you please drive the boys to the hospital?"

Summer nodded, the giant lump in her throat preventing her from answering.

"Good. We need to talk later." Her heart dropped at his curt words. She was going to be fired.

Holden jumped into the ambulance and they all stood, watching it leave. The sorrow on their faces brought tears to her eyes which she quickly wiped away.

"Where are the keys?"

Mark ran into the house while Luke and John sped toward the truck. Silence and tension stretched through the whole trip. She could tell they were each trying to remain calm in their own way. They finally pulled into the hospital parking lot, parked and headed toward the emergency room.

One look at Holden's worried face caused her chest to squeeze. He gave them all a feeble smile. He sat in a plastic chair that looked so uncomfortable and too small for his large frame. John immediately sat next to him and put his arms around Holden. Holden cradled John's head against his shoulder.

"Is he going to be all right?" Luke whispered.

Holden nodded absently. "They haven't come out to talk to me yet."

Luke nodded and sat down next to John.

Her heart broke for all of them. The worry in their eyes and the frowns on their faces made her ache for them.

Mark sighed heavily. "Holden, it's my fault. I should have made sure that no one messed with Yukon. I was cleaning out Yukon's stall and I should have kept a better eye out." His voice broke and faded.

Holden flashed her a hard look and she wondered if she should leave. This was a place for the family to be together and she wasn't part of the family. The blame lay on her shoulders and she had to wrap her arms around her middle to keep from coming undone.

The aging doctor walked into the dour room, toward Holden, and smiled. "A broken ankle but from the x-rays it appears as though Matt has had broken bones before. Goes with the territory I guess." He winked at John. "Cowboys are tough. Your brother will be fine. He'll probably drive you nuts before he's completely healed but I want him off that foot."

John let go of Holden. "I'll keep an eye on him."

The doctor smiled again. "That's what I thought. He's asking to see Summer."

Her face warmed as she locked eyes with Holden. His anger was visibly smoldering. "No, Holden should be the one to see him. Tell him I'll see him at home." Clutching her purse, she walked out of the hospital, wondering if she would still have a job. Getting into the truck, she wondered if she should have gone to see Matt. Damned if she did. Damned if she didn't. She started the truck and was surprised when Holden came running out.

"Wait. We have no way to get home if you take the truck."

"I'm sorry. I'm so upset about Matt. I wasn't thinking."

"Mark is in with Matt now. He'll be right out to go with you and then drive the truck back here." He left before she had a chance to say anything else.

If he had wanted her to stay he would have said so. Guilt racked her and doubt filled her. It wasn't just her job she worried about, it was the boys. She got out of the truck and switched to the passenger side.

Mark came out and jumped into the truck. They didn't say a thing the whole ride. He stopped in front of the house and sat staring straight ahead until she got out.

A tear spilled over as she watched him drive away and she quickly dashed it away. The only way for her to get through this was to keep herself busy. There were beds to make and things to clean. They'd want something warm to eat when they got home too.

As she got closer to the house she spotted Yukon. He was roaming around free outside the fence. Now what? Horses didn't frighten her since she'd grown up on a small ranch. But Yukon had the look of the devil in his eyes. He ran and turned and ran and turned. There was no way she was going to catch him.

Yukon put himself between her and the front door. Damn why couldn't anything go right? Her heart beat faster as she tried to gauge her next move. One glance toward the clothes lines had her abruptly sputtering with anger. Every sheet lay on the ground "You mangy horse, I guess you don't care that we need those sheets tonight!"

Yukon stopped and stared at her. He appeared to be sizing her up. He stood perfectly still, watching her.

If she made a run for it, would he come after her? What was he doing? She stared back. Perspiration formed on her brow and she wiped it away with her sleeve. Damn, damn, damn.

"Okay, come and get me. I have too much to do today and it's too damn hot out here for me to play games with you."

Yukon just stared. She had to admit the bay was beautiful. She could sense the power he held. He knew it too.

"Listen, Yukon, I need to get inside. Don't you think you've caused enough trouble for one day?"

The horse gave her one last look and cantered away, toward the unfenced pastures.

This was her chance and she was taking it. She ran into the house and slammed the door closed. The house was blissfully cool.

She'd have to call someone about the horse though. Picking up the phone, she dialed the O'Malleys. Thankfully Caleb answered and promised to come.

One crisis at a time, she supposed. While she waited, she had time to feel guilty about Matt's fall and to worry about Holden's stone cold glances. If worse came to worse, she'd ask for a day's pay and hightail it out of there. With gas being so expensive, she wasn't sure how far she'd be able to go but it would have to do.

Relief washed over her when Caleb finally pulled his truck up to the house. He was as gorgeous as ever. Tall, dark, and handsome with the cutest dimple in his left cheek. He also had the longest eyelashes she had ever seen. Women always sighed when they saw him. His grin was always the same, shit eatin'. He attended college in Texas and hadn't been back long. Summer break just started.

She waved to him from the window and sighed when he tipped his gray Stetson to her. He looked all business staring at Yukon. Caleb's talent at roping was legendary but as she watched him take his fifth try she wondered if it was true. Yukon led him on a merry chase and finally Caleb roped him. A struggle of wills started but Caleb came out the winner. Yukon was a smart and strong contender. As soon as Yukon was secure, she opened the door and stepped outside.

"Sure am glad you were home." She smiled at him.

"I heard you were out here. How's it going?"

Her shoulders slumped. "To tell you the truth, I'm waiting for Holden to get back and fire me."

"Now why would he do that?" The Texas drawl he picked up at school made him even more appealing.

"Aren't you going to call me darlin' or honey pie?"

Caleb blinked, appearing baffled.

Summer laughed. "Isn't that what all the Texans call women?"

Caleb chuckled. "Depends. Darlin' is fine. Honey pie would probably be a reason to get slapped. Tell me what happened with Matt and Yukon. You didn't say how Matt got hurt when you called."

"He was doing something with Yukon and ended up with a busted ankle. I'm supposed to watch them. Holden was napping and I was making lunch. It's a big mess and I'm pretty sure that Holden blames me." Her arms dropped to her sides and her shoulders slumped.

"Hey, honey pie, don't let it get you down." Caleb didn't get the expected smile from the endearment. "Holden seems like a good, fair man. I'm sure it shocked and worried him that Matt got hurt. It's not your fault. Happens to the best of us. Hell, it's part of working a ranch."

She relaxed for a minute. "Thanks for trying to make me feel better."

"You've had a hard time of it I hear. Tell you what, if Holden gives you a problem, you're welcome over at our place. Can't really pay much, but if you're in a bind, we'd love to have you."

Summer reached up and gave Caleb a big hug. His arms felt strong and protective around her. She wished there was chemistry between them. He was possibly the nicest man she knew.

The honking of a truck horn pulling up broke them apart and they stood together while Holden parked his truck.

Half afraid that he was going to fire her, she bit her

bottom lip so hard, she tasted blood. Stone cold, that's what Holden's expression was and it unnerved her. "How's Matt?"

Holden ignored her and shook hands with Caleb. "What brings you out here?" His aim to sound jovial missed its mark. "Obviously you two know each other."

Caleb smiled. "Grew up in the same town. You could say we know each other."

Holden's eyes narrowed. "Is this a social visit?"

"Oh for Pete's sake. Yukon was out when I got home and he barely let me in the house. I called the O'Malleys place looking for help. I didn't want to distract you from being with Matt." Summer crossed her arms and glared at Holden. "You should be thanking Caleb instead of grilling him. I take full responsibility for Matt's injury and if you want me gone just say so." She held her breath, waiting.

Mark, Luke and John finally joined them, all wide eyed and silent.

Caleb took a step toward Holden. "Now wait a minute. I came out here to do a favor, not to cause trouble. Now if you're going to give honey pie a hard time, I'm taking her with me."

Summer couldn't help it. Nervous laughter bubbled up inside her and she had to put her hand over her mouth to make it stop. Caleb winked at her making it harder to look serious.

The glare Holden gave Caleb put an instant stop to her laughter. "I don't know what's going on here but Summer works for me."

"It doesn't seem like I'm making any friends here. The honey pie thing was a joke. Summer has had a hard time of it. Treat her right, okay?"

Holden nodded still frowning. He held out his hand to Caleb. "Thanks for your help, Caleb," he said as they shook.

"I'm out of here. Beautiful horse by the way." Caleb

winked at Summer and smiled at the boys before making a beeline for his truck.

What a charmer. She didn't realize how big her smile was until she noticed Holden's steely stare. Her smile withered under his scrutiny.

"Boys, why don't y'all go inside? I bet Summer has some food ready."

"It's all ready just help yourself." The sweet "I don't care" tone of voice that she strived for didn't happen. It sounded more like a worried croak.

The boys hesitated, looking at both of them. The worry in their eyes fired her up. She might feel guilty, but she wasn't going without setting Holden straight.

The boys went into the house and Summer turned, staring directly into Holden's dark eyes. She was ready for a fight but the misery she glimpsed there melted her heart. "How's Matt?" She was glad she sounded compassionate instead of croaky this time.

"He'll be fine."

"You're upset with me. I know it's my job to watch them but quite frankly I did the best I could. I was in and out of the house all morning and I was making lunch when it all happened. I feel awful. If you want me out of here, I understand." She bit her lip again waiting for an answer. Her poor lip was so sore.

"Is that what you want? Do you want to be with Caleb?" He glanced away, staring out toward the mountains.

"No, of course not. He's a friend. I know Colt too. Caleb is always taking in strays and I suppose he saw me as a stray. I don't want or need that type of entanglement. Men are off the menu as far as I'm concerned."

He took a deep breath and let it go. Turning toward her, he studied her as though he could see her soul. "It wasn't your fault. Matt knew better and his brothers told him not to. I'm starved." He left her standing there without another word.

Somehow she felt cheated. Where was the offer to stay? Where was the question about not wanting entanglements? Heck, she should be glad that he hadn't sent her packing. Holden O'Leary was an infuriating, confusing, yet caring man, and she'd probably never understand him. She wanted to tell him about the robbery at the bar and grill, but now wasn't the time. Hopefully an opportune moment would crop up soon. He needed to hear it from her first.

CHAPTER THREE

*H*olden helped Matt into the house, leading him to the freshly made up couch. Matt objected and tried to steer away from it. "I'm no cripple." Holden sighed. It was going to be a very long weekend.

The doctor ordered Matt to stay off his feet for a while before he could use crutches. But Matt wasn't the most patient of people.

Summer walked into the great room with a wide smile for Matt. Holden wasn't on the receiving end of any smiles from her, but at least she had stopped scowling at him.

Watching her last night with Mark, Luke and John had been enlightening. She soothed their worries and their guilt. She gave them the tender care they'd been missing since their parents died. He wasn't sure what to do. It was unimaginable she was capable of being an accomplice in a robbery, let alone murder, but according to Beverly, a lot of people believed her guilty. What about the guy who did rob and beat them? Where was he? He couldn't remember if Beverly had shared that little tidbit with him.

"Tell me your favorite foods, Matt." Again, she had a great big smile for Matt.

"My favorite is homemade mac and cheese. I also like baked ham and sweet potatoes. I like eggs with bacon. And—"

"I think she gets the idea." Holden chuckled. His phone rang. He was needed in the office. "Summer, I'm going to leave you some money so you can get groceries. Don't worry about the boys. I'll have John stay with Matt while Mark and Luke get some work done."

Doubt and something he couldn't decipher were in her eyes. "It'll be fine." He handed her two one hundred dollar bills and laughed when her eyes widened and eyebrows rose. "What? We eat a lot."

She nodded. He could sense her reluctance but didn't have time to dwell on it. Someone with a sick dog was at the clinic.

Even during the drive he still couldn't get her out of his mind. In the short time he'd spent with her he'd come to admire her. The kindness she showed his brothers was beyond her job description. Even if she couldn't stand him, he liked her well enough. Maybe more than just well enough. When he parked, he said a quick prayer of thankfulness that Beverly Rain wasn't waiting for him. He rushed into the office and was instantly in Vet mode.

The little Chihuahua, named Tiny, required surgery on its knee cap. Mindy Sue certainly impressed him as she helped him and her pink hair was so outrageous today, he smiled.

It warmed his insides when he later reassured Mrs. Beasley, Tiny's thankful owner. She bubbled over with gratitude, then grabbed his cheeks and kissed him on the lips. Holden wanted to gag but he was a professional. As soon as she left Mindy Sue broke out in laughter and handed him a bottle of mouthwash she kept in her desk drawer. He grabbed the bottle and headed into the bathroom to rinse his mouth.

"Doc, come quick," Mindy Sue called seconds later.

Holden quickly dried his hands and raced to the waiting room. The sheriff stood in the middle of the room with his feet planted shoulder width apart. Beady brown eyes stared him down. He hoped it wasn't his brothers.

"Sheriff, what a nice surprise."

"Brown, Sheriff Brown and this is not a social visit." He took off his cap and scratched his head. He wore a military style crew cut. "Do you know Summer Louise Fitzgerald?"

"Yes, what's this all about?"

"She claims you gave her two, one hundred dollar bills but I think the money is from the recent robbery she is suspected to be involved in. I've been biding my time waiting for her to make a mistake." He held up the two one hundred dollar bills.

Holden's jaw dropped. "Her claim is the truth. I gave her the money to buy groceries with. Where is she?"

The sheriff's eyes narrowed. "She wouldn't be doing anything illegal to earn this money would she?"

Holden's body stiffened as he clenched his hands. "No. She works for me, end of story. I'd like my money back and I demand to know where Summer is."

The disappointment on the sheriff's face amazed Holden. "She's in a cell."

"What?" The urge to punch first and talk later was strong. He grabbed his Stetson and locked gazes with Mindy Sue "Call if you need me. I might as well find out where the local jail is." Wide eyed, Mindy Sue nodded.

Holden didn't talk to the sheriff the whole way to the jail. He just stalked behind him, fuming. If there had been one shred of proof, he had no doubt that Summer would have been arrested and charged.

Following the sheriff into the police station, he frowned. The jail was tiny with two holding cells. Summer's arms were crossed across her chest and she appeared gloriously defiant sitting on the bench in one of the cells.

Sheriff Brown opened the cell and waved her out. "You don't want to get mixed up with the likes of her, Doc. It'll only bring you misery in the end. Oh and don't get too attached to her either. She'll end up behind bars where she belongs soon enough."

Holden grabbed Summer's hand as soon as she opened her mouth. "Let's get out of here," he murmured.

She closed her mouth and held on to his hand as he led them out of the police station. "Thank you for coming to get me."

He stopped outside the door and gazed at her hardened face. "Did you have doubts?"

"No one ever came to get me before."

He wrapped her in his arms and pulled her to him. No matter what life threw at him he always had his brothers but she had no one, it seemed. Her softness against him stirred him and his heart began to beat faster. The scent of vanilla filled him. It was a scent he was beginning to crave.

Summer pulled away. "Please, not here. People already have the wrong idea of me. I don't want them to think badly of you."

"I don't care what they think."

Her sad smile melted his heart. "You will eventually. I wasn't able to get the groceries by the way. I had them all in the cart and when I tried to pay all hell broke loose."

He took his phone out of his pocket and called Mindy Sue, asking her to pick up the groceries if they were still in the cart and giving her a short list to grab if they weren't. Hanging up, he took Summer's hand. "Let's go home."

"I'll meet you there."

"Oh no, I'm not letting you go." He stood firm.

"What about the truck? Surely you don't want to leave it in town."

He gave her hand a light squeeze. "I'll have Mark get it next time I come to town, which by the way is too often. I'm thinking about getting another receptionist and having Mindy Sue as my tech full time. I want to pay for her to go back to school. She's a natural with animals and we need more than one vet around here."

"You have been busy."

"We'll see what I can work out." He opened her door for her and it amused him when her lips parted forming an "o".

Sliding into his seat he tried to give her a reassuring grin. Her eyes teared up, but she didn't cry. She was tough and fragile both, in her own way. He liked that about her.

The drive home was silent. He figured she needed to gather her thoughts. He'd been mulling over the whole scene himself. He needed to talk to her about it, to know the whole story so he could help.

Soon enough they were home. While they walked to the house side by side, he wished he had some words that would make her feel better.

He reached for the doorknob and felt her gentle hand on his arm. Turning he gazed into her sad blue eyes.

"Thank you again for coming to get me." She took a deep breath, let it out, and put a slight smile on her face. "I hope Matt is still on the couch resting." Her shoulders straightened as she preceded him into the house.

THE BOYS WERE CONFUSED about why she didn't come home with groceries and were a bit put out when they didn't get any answers. They were even more confused when Mindy Sue showed up with the food later. Summer almost didn't recognize her with pink hair and plaid nails. Envy washed over her as she watched Mindy Sue's easy way with people. She had all the boys eating out of her hand.

Gazing at Holden, Summer noticed that he was entranced by her too. Maybe Holden was the type that liked pink hair. She really didn't know him enough to say. Hadn't he mentioned something about paying for Mindy Sue to go to school?

Summer put the groceries away and tried to smile as she thanked Mindy Sue. Her already heavy heart grew weighty when Holden walked Mindy Sue out to her car. It wasn't any of her business. She hardly knew Holden and if he was dating Mindy Sue then so be it. She was here to work.

She couldn't help herself. She walked to the window and watched Holden and Mindy Sue talking. It did matter, she conceded, but there was nothing she could do about it. Any chance she'd had ended the moment Sheriff Brown arrested her. Trembling, she turned away and went back to setting the kitchen to rights.

Homemade mac and cheese was in order. She needed the comfort food as much as Matt did. Glancing over at Matt she found that he switched around on the couch so that he could watch her.

"Did you get along well enough while I was in town?"

Matt nodded. "I suppose, but I sure am glad that you're here."

"That's so sweet."

Matt scowled. "I'm not a child you know."

"I know." She turned back to the kitchen counter. Matt was trying so hard to prove he was all grown up. She never had a choice. She was a girl one day and a grown up the next. The accident that took her parents left her on her own. If the whole robbery hadn't have happened she would have been proud of her success in keeping a roof over her head. Now the pride was gone.

The front door opened and closed. Summer didn't turn around, continuing to grate the cheddar cheese. Soon enough she could feel the heat of him behind her. He breathed on the back of her neck sending a shiver down her spine.

"I'm making mac and cheese." It sounded lame to her.

He stepped closer until his body barely touched hers. "I see that. Smells good."

Turning her head slightly, she saw the side of his face as he looked over her shoulder.

"What are you doing?" Matt sounded angry.

Summer instantly straightened, but Holden was extremely slow at stepping back. "Making dinner is all." Her voice wavered.

As Holden stepped away, she instantly missed his nearness and she knew she was a fool. Who'd want to be with her, the suspected accomplice? Besides he seemed to have his eye on Mindy Sue.

Holden took her hand in his big, strong one. "We'll talk about the sheriff later."

She gazed into his eyes trying to read him. He confused her to no end. She couldn't tell what he was thinking. Hell, she barely knew him and she needed to get a grip on her wayward emotions. "Fine."

He let go of her hand and ambled over to Matt. He sat in a chair next to the couch and the two talked in low tones. Neither one looked at her, so she ignored them and concentrated on cooking.

The thought of talking later interfered with her focus.

Would she still have a job? It amazed her that she no longer felt the fear of being jobless. Caleb took care of that. It was the power of her feelings for Holden that worried her the most.

Dinner was jovial with the boys all teasing Matt about how much work they have to do with him laid up. Summer did not look at Holden at all. She could feel the heat of his gaze, but she needed to be in self-preservation mode. It was bound to hurt when he told her to leave. In the short time she'd been there she'd grown attached to all of the O'Learys. Who'd want a suspect in their house anyway? Holden needed to do what was best for his family and the best thing would be for her to go.

Yet, he had touched her in the kitchen. Her thoughts whirled as she pushed the food around on her plate. The boys didn't seem to notice how upset she felt. She gave them half smiles and half answers. The end of the meal couldn't come fast enough.

Clearing the table and washing the dishes with Holden watching unnerved her. She finished, turned around and there stood Holden with her coat in his hand.

"Am I going somewhere?" She bit her sore bottom lip.

"I don't have an office, I thought we could take a walk together."

Summer grabbed her coat and avoided his stare. "A walk would be just fine." A lump formed in her throat and she wondered if she should have grabbed some tissues. She followed him outside.

Bright stars peeked out and the moon glowed. The cooler air felt wonderful and the backdrop of the mountains made for a spectacular view. They walked toward the open green pastures, side by side and the silence made her feel awkward. Holden stopped finally and took her hand. "We need to talk."

"Yes, you mentioned that." This was it. He was going to

ask her to leave. She didn't want to go but she'd known all along it was inevitable.

"Will you tell me about what was going on with the sheriff?"

The fact that he asked her instead of demanding that she explain helped her to breathe easier. She cleared her throat and looked out toward the mountains. "It's a complicated story. I grew up on a small ranch. I lived there until my parents died. My dad loved to fish and my mother often went along. We don't know what happened but they drowned and their bodies were found on the bank of the lake." She drew her hand from his and clasped both her hands together. "Ranch life, my home, it was all an illusion. We didn't really own anything but the clothes on our backs. I never knew. By the time everything was auctioned and sold, I barely settled all the debt. Paul Gallagher, a friend of my dad's, offered me a job and gave me a place to live. He became like a father to me. I bartended at his Bar and Grill and he taught me how to cook."

She closed her eyes and took a deep breath, grateful that Holden hadn't interrupted. "I worked for him for three years. I made enough money to pay my bills. I didn't really date much. My schedule wasn't the best for a relationship. Then one day a cowboy named Brent walked into the bar. He seemed nice enough. He never got fresh, never started a fight. We'd talk. I dated him for exactly one month but he had me fooled. Even when we broke up, I still thought of him as a nice man."

"Why'd you break up?"

"My schedule. You know how it is. He had to be up with the sun and that was when I was going to bed. It wasn't a bad break up, it just was. I saw him around town and we were fine. It was just the timing. Two months ago near closing time he came in to say hi. I hadn't a clue that he was evil. He was the last one in the bar so I walked with him to the door, keys in hand ready to lock up. He slapped me across the face so hard that I fell and he grabbed the keys and locked the door."

"Summer, I'm so sorry."

"Please, Holden, don't say anything or I won't be able to get the story out."

Holden nodded and quieted.

"Paul came from behind the bar with a baseball bat in his hands and Brent pulled a gun on him, taking the bat from Paul. He had a hold on the back of my hair and I couldn't get free. He made us stand against the wall while he ripped the phones out. I tried to run for the stairs and he pistol whipped me in the face. He used the bat to viciously beat Paul. The screams became groans, then nothing. Blood was everywhere and I could see that Paul was dead. He had me open the safe and the cash register. He wanted to know where the rest of the money was. I told him we go to the bank every morning."

"You don't have to tell me the rest."

"No, I want you to hear my side of the whole story. He dragged me upstairs and hit me a few more times. The next thing I knew the sheriff was there and I was pretty much naked. He didn't even cover me while he waited for the ambulance. Creeps me out to know he was looking at me. They never caught Brent but the sheriff was sure that I was involved. You know why? This is the kicker. I was involved because I wasn't raped. I was only beaten."

Holden opened his big strong arms to her and she gladly stepped into the comfort he offered. It had been so long since anyone had believed her. He did believe her, didn't he? The need to know outweighed the comfort of his arms. Pulling back, she saw worry and compassion in his dark eyes.

"You believe me?" Someone had told her once not to ask

questions you don't want the answer to. Her body suddenly chilled and her chin wobbled.

"Of course I believe you. You are a victim, Summer, and I don't understand how everyone knew all the details. There are privacy laws now."

"Not if your name is Beverly. I think the sheriff has a thing for her. She is always bringing him cakes and pies."

A smile crossed Holden's face and he chuckled. "I know it's not funny but I can't imagine those two together. The thought gives me nightmares." He pulled her back into his arms and cradled her head against his chest with his palm. He kissed the top of her head.

Summer gazed up at him. His eyes glittered in the moonlight. The desire she saw was unmistakable. Yearning surged through her. The beating of her heart grew faster as his head inch down until his delectable lips were against hers. She reached up and wrapped her arms around his neck as he pulled her flush against him. The kiss grew bolder and she opened for him. His kiss was powerful and she felt weak in the knees.

Suddenly, Holden stepped back and the words unfair and wow came to mind.

"The door just slammed. One of my brothers is around."

She nodded and smiled at Holden's shortness of breath. She seemed to have the same effect on him.

Luke walked over toward them and Holden took a big step away from her. "Hey, Luke. What's up?" Holden gave his brother a smile.

Luke shrugged his shoulder and gave Summer a hard look. "Matt's asking for you both. Well, either one would probably do."

"Is something wrong with him?" Guilt washed over her. She should have been in the house taking care of him.

"Don't rightly know."

"Thanks for the walk, Holden. You're right I do need to take more walks." Summer strode away and hurried to the house. What had she been thinking? Good Lord, how dense could she get? Holden did not need to get mixed up with the likes of her.

CHAPTER FOUR

The next morning Holden's body wanted Summer while his mind tried to deny the attraction.

He had Matt to consider. Last night when he walked into the house Matt stared at him with disgust. He'd suspected that Matt had a crush on Summer, but he didn't realize how big of a crush.

It seemed as though there was always someone else to consider. That's what families did, but for once couldn't it be his turn to be selfish, his turn to love?

The heavenly scent of coffee wafted up the stairs. Real coffee, not the instant stuff he usually made on the go.

Energized from a full night's sleep, he got out of bed looking forward to the day and quickly dressed.

He started downstairs and stopped on the bottom step. Summer's smile illuminated the whole kitchen. He could hear her soft humming. Grinning, he walked to the kitchen and caught her gaze. There was definitely something between them. Her eyes twinkled as she blushed and he felt like a teenager again, an awkward one but somehow it was fine.

"Take a picture it lasts longer." There was no missing the sarcasm in Matt's voice.

"Morning, Matt. How are you feeling today?" Holden went over and ruffled his hair for which he got a glare. He sat in the leather chair next to the couch.

"Coffee?" Summer asked from the kitchen.

Matt answered first. "That would be most kind of you, Summer"

"Holden, I know you take yours black. Matt, how about you?"

"As black as you can make it."

Holden wanted to laugh. Matt always poured tons of sugar in his and a big portion of milk. Matt's scowl seemed permanent. In fact he completely ignored Holden.

"Matt, how did you sleep?"

Matt stared at him. "I closed my eyes, you know the usual way."

"Any pain?" Holden took a deep breath and slowly let it out.

"My ankle is busted. What do you think?" Matt turned red when he noticed that Summer stood behind him listening.

"Here, Matt." She handed him his coffee. "I get a bit cranky before I've had my coffee too." She handed Holden his mug and returned to the kitchen. "I'll have breakfast ready in a flash."

Matt took a sip of his coffee and almost gagged. His eyes flashed at Holden. "How do you drink it like this?"

"When I started drinking coffee, we rarely had sugar in the house and never any milk."

"When we lived with Mom?"

Holden nodded. "A long time ago."

"Holden, why do you think she did it? Was she mad at us? Did we make her life miserable?"

Holden's heart twisted. He never asked about their mother before. "No Matt. It wasn't any of us. She loved us. When Dad left she sank into a depression that she never got out of. She tried to raise us herself. I don't know who gave her the drugs she OD'd on. I tried to find out but they were some really nasty people. Eventually I had to quit looking."

Matt nodded. "I wish we knew where Dad went."

Holden shook his head. "We're better off without him. He used to hit Mom."

Matt's brows furrowed. "I never knew."

"Don't tell the others. I don't want them to remember how it was. I'm just glad I was old enough to be your guardian. They would have split you up for sure."

Matt didn't scowl at him now. In fact he appeared almost grateful.

The rest of the boys came clambering down the stairs for breakfast making conversation impossible. Holden watched Summer as she greeted each one and asked questions pertinent to each boy. Holden's heart grew, taking in each smile, each touch on the shoulder, and each laugh. It had been a long time coming but maybe they found happiness.

Uprooting them from school and their friends had been gut wrenchingly hard. It had been a long road after his mother died, but watching the boys smiling made every sacrifice worth it.

"Holden, do you want to eat over there with Matt?" Summer asked, her eyes sparkling.

"If it's no trouble."

"Not at all. Give me a minute to sort these young men out and I'll make us something."

Holden saw Matt peering at him then at Summer. This time there wasn't a scowl. His brothers made quick work of breakfast, then Mark led the charge outside with Luke and John right behind him.

"Stay away from Yukon!" Holden heard something about stupid before they closed the door.

Summer carried over three plates piled high with eggs, bacon and toast. She set them down before she went back to grab her coffee, bringing the pot with her. "Refills?"

Matt's eyes grew wide. "I usually only have one cup."

Holden suppressed the chuckled that was trying to escape. "I'll have more, thanks, Summer."

"Is it a big secret or can you tell me what went on yester-day?" Matt asked.

Summer turned an enticing shade of red and she gave Holden a quick glance. Panic was written all over her face.

"Sure, you need to know." Holden started.

"Holden—"

"It's fine, Summer, Matt needs to know the situation in case Brent comes around."

Summer appeared doubtful but she nodded.

"Here it is in a nutshell. Summer dated some yahoo, who after they broke up, robbed and killed the owner of the place Summer worked at. She was beaten pretty badly and there are some people in town that think that she had a part in it."

Matt sat up, wincing. "There's no way you'd be a part of anything like that."

Summer gave him a half smile. "Thanks for the vote of confidence, Matt. Brent got away. I don't expect him back. But you do need to know that some people will not be friendly to you because of me."

"We need to know what this ass looks like so we can all be on the lookout. What happened in town yesterday?" Matt appeared more than ready to take on the world.

"I went grocery shopping and when I checked out, the cashier took the money your brother gave me and handed it to the manager who called for the sheriff. Sheriff Brown was conveniently in the manager's office. They must have called him as soon as I set foot in the store. Anyway, I was taken in for questioning. That sheriff is very nasty and wholly convinced I was part of the murder and robbery. He went and verified my story with Holden. Holden came and took me home."

Matt whistled through his teeth. "Wow. I'm glad you're here. We can protect you."

A warm glow flowed through Holden. Home, Summer had called this place home. "Do you have a picture of Brent?"

"No, I don't. I bet the sheriff has one. If he'd be willing to share, that I don't know." She pushed her food around her plate, barely eating. Finally, she stood up and grabbed their empty plates and went to the kitchen.

Matt turned to Holden. "I'm sorry I got all bent out of shape. A minor crush is all. It's nothing like what happened in Texas."

Holden stood and put his hand on Matt's shoulder. "Not at all. Summer is a good woman."

Matt nodded and Holden grabbed their mugs and carried them into the kitchen. It amazed him that in a few short days, the kitchen had become such a warm welcoming place. It could all be attributed to Summer. No, Summer was not like that woman in Texas. Summer would never pit brother against brother.

———

A LOT HAD HAPPENED in the last twenty-four hours but the only thing worth remembering was Holden's kiss. Never in her life had she thought a kiss could affect her so. It had been a brain numbing, spine tingling, knee weakening, heart pounding kiss. Lord, she wanted more. There'd been the promise of more in his hard response to her. What was happening to her? Just knowing what was in his jeans made her crazy with desire.

Holden hadn't gone into the office and she'd swear that every time she looked up he was studying her. It unnerved her. She wanted him that much was obvious, but was it too soon? Employer/employee relationships were never a good idea. And could she truly trust a man again? Most of all she didn't want to harm his reputation.

"Do you need anything, Matt?"

"No, I could use some company though."

Smiling, she sat in the chair next to him. "Is your ankle bothering you?"

"A bit. I'm going stir crazy. We have practically a million channels on TV and still there is nothing on."

"I know what you mean. I worked nights and I never found too much to watch during the day. Maybe you could read a book?"

Matt groaned. "No. I wouldn't mind a few magazines from the store but I don't want you to go and get them."

"It's fine Matt. I'm sure Holden can pick them up next time he's in town or maybe Mindy Sue can drop them by."

Nodding, he gave her a lopsided grin. "Mindy Sue sure is a looker. I love that I never know what color her hair will be. A real unique woman and Holden says she's a gem. He's going to pay for her to go to college so she can be his partner. He must be mighty impressed with her. They do spend long hours together."

The high she'd felt all day started to diminish with every word. A shroud of loneliness covered her. What a fool she was. Hard learned life lessons hadn't really been learned at all. It took a handsome cowboy with a powerfully sexy kiss to turn her head. A smack to the head is what she needed to wake her up to her reality. Of course Holden would like Mindy Sue. It sounded as though they had a lot in common.

"Is something wrong?"

Summer gave Matt her full attention and smiled. "No, I was just thinking. What is the story with that ornery horse anyway?"

"Yukon? Not much to tell. He isn't a rescue horse. He just hasn't learned his manners is all. He's a stallion and a bit aggressive."

"Do you plan to use him for breeding?"

Matt young face turned red. "He's going to be one of our strong bloodlines. Holden bought prime stock before we moved here. A new start and all and I shouldn't have messed with that horse. I knew better."

"Glad to hear that," Holden's voice boomed.

Startled, Summer turned toward Holden. Much to her dismay, her body immediately reacted. It was going to take a lot of work to keep her body in check after that kiss. She didn't even know if it was possible. This morning she cherished such reactions, now they horrified her. She wasn't sure what his game was but she didn't intend on playing.

Holden took the seat opposite her and gave her a slow sexy grin. His eyes lit up and she swore she saw desire in them.

"Holden, I'm glad you're here. I have a ton to do. Maybe you could keep Matt entertained for a while?"

Holden's eyebrow rose as he stared at her. "That's why I came in."

Summer quickly nodded, got up out of the chair and headed up the stairs. What a fool, somehow she never got anything right. Holden must think she expected him to be in the house just to see her. She sat on her bed while anger bubbled inside. When had she begun to act like a teenager with her first crush? She only worked here and it would do her good to remember that. Most men made her nervous after what happened at the bar and grill but Holden made her feel protected.

But Mindy Sue was a better choice for him. They worked together, she loved animals and she was a good person. She drew in a shaky breath; the anger didn't erase the hurt. She needed to buck up. There was no room in her screwed up life for romance and as much as she wanted to stay hidden in her room, she had five hungry mouths to feed.

Barbeque chicken, baked beans, biscuits and mashed potatoes were on the menu. It was more than enough to keep her busy. She got off the bed and viewed herself in the mirror. She'd never been a beauty but she didn't like how pale she appeared. To add some color to her cheeks, she lightly squeezed them. She took a deep breath and pretended to be happy.

DINNER WAS delicious but if he lived to be a hundred he'd still never understand females. No matter what he did, he couldn't get a smile out of Summer. Well, she smiled but it was a fake smile and he hated it. He knew her true smile and he yearned to see it again.

All through dinner she refused to glance his way. His heart did a two-step whenever she was near and quite frankly it hurt that she ignored him. Last night, kissing her had been magic. Now she made it clear she wanted nothing to do with him. What could have changed in such little time?

He watched her clean the kitchen and he couldn't take it anymore. Grabbing his hat he mumbled something about checking on the horses and lit out. The fresh air was welcome. The horses needed tending and Yukon needed to be talked to. The ornery Stallion allowed only him to come close.

Yukon had trust issues. Maybe he had a fickle female in his past. That, Holden understood. Summer probably just wanted to keep her job, but the passion they shared blew his mind. Maybe it wasn't as shared as he thought. Perhaps he was the only one who felt it. Hell, what did he really know about women? Summer had gotten under his skin and now it was going to take a lot of self-control to avoid her. He had enough to do with raising his brothers and building his practice. Today had been a rarity day since he hadn't been called in. All must have been well in the animal world.

The barn beckoned him and in he went, ambling down to Yukon's stall. What a magnificent animal, a beautiful Bay. A lot of dreams were wrapped up in him. He came from a long line of winners. Maybe he should have called Colt to take a look. Colt had a way of communicating with horses that Holden envied.

Surprisingly, Yukon came over to the stall gate. He stared at Holden then snorted, shaking his head. Holden chuckled. "I don't think it's so much that you're ornery. I think you're full of personality. Once you learn your manners you'll have a harem of the most beautiful women."

"He doesn't know what you're sayin'," Luke commented as he approached Holden.

Holden smiled down at Luke. "I think he does."

Luke cocked his head to one side studying Holden. "Maybe he knows that girls are just trouble."

"Why would you say to that?"

Luke rolled his eyes. "Like you have to ask? You know I'm not stupid don't cha?"

"Of course you're not stupid. Where is this going, Luke?"

Luke frowned. "We had to leave Texas because of a woman. Now Matt is all gaga over Summer and ends up hurting himself. I saw you kissing her. She's a thief in case you hadn't heard. What happened to bros before hos?"

Holden's mouth dropped open. "First of all, Summer is not a ho. Second of all, women are to be respected. Thirdly, she is not a thief."

Luke put his hands over his ears. A look of disgust crossed his features.

"What?"

"I've heard it all before. Same song different girl. I thought our focus was to keep our noses clean and stay together. I'm not going to some foster home because she shakes her ass at you."

"She does not." Holden sighed. "Listen it's not like that. The four of you mean everything to me."

"Sure until Summer shakes her—"

"Luke, don't even say it. I thought you liked Summer."

Luke shook his head glumly. "Not anymore. She's trouble."

"Listen—"

"No, you listen. I won't give her a hard time but I won't like it. You think Matt is done being all gaga over her? Take a good look. We moved here for a calm life." Luke glared at him before turning around and stomping out of the barn.

Holden ran his hand through his hair. Luke had a point. They did move to have a drama free life and here he was in the thick of it again. His brothers did come first and his libido had to come last. Maybe once they were all adults he'd be able to pursue a relationship but not now.

But she still made his blood hot. A wave of loneliness settled over him. He'd get over it. Other single parents made the same sacrifice and in essence that is what he was, a single parent.

Yukon poked his head out over the gate giving Holden a baleful look. "You too? Can't a guy get a break?"

Yukon snorted at him again and pulled his head back into the stall.

CHAPTER FIVE

*T*he next few days were hectic, and Summer tried to keep up with it all. Holden was called to so many emergencies she began to think of the front door as revolving. He'd been in a bad mood too. He hadn't even thanked her for breakfast this morning.

Matt had suddenly turned helpless and needy. He needed her constant presence and it wore on her. He was as moody as Holden.

Luke for some reason decided that he hated her. How many different glares were there? He'd sent them all her way. It was decidedly uncomfortable and a bit alarming.

Mark was busy taking charge. He came in for his meals and was polite to her each time.

John was the only normal one in the bunch. He laughed and made jokes. He smiled and carried on conversations with her. At least he still seemed to like her.

If it wasn't for the fact that they needed someone to cook and clean she'd have left. Well, she had to admit it was being needed for more than a housekeeper that kept her there. The boys hungered for attention in their own way. Maybe Luke would come around. Her mother had always told her that nothing worth having was ever easy. Summer smiled and shook her head. This was in no way easy.

A car came up the drive. Summer glanced out the window and recognized Mindy Sue's beat up, red, two-door car. Holden wasn't at home so she wondered what Mindy Sue wanted.

Summer was on her way to the front door when Matt told her to hurry up. Some days a good smack seemed in order, but that wasn't her way. She opened the door and Mindy Sue smiled at her. Her hair was jet black and waist length and her fingernails were gold and black today. Summer had to admit that Mindy Sue was very attractive.

"Hi, Summer! Holden sent me out here with some magazines for Matt." She walked into the house with a spring in her step.

"Matt's on the couch." Summer didn't even know why she bothered to say that. Mindy Sue could see Matt from the door.

Mindy Sue was perky. She was probably one of those people that woke up singing. Summer had to concede that she was nice enough. Holden had his eye on Mindy Sue and why not? They had the world in common and she'd be the perfect helpmate for him. According to everyone, Holden was going to pay for Mindy to go back to school. Every time she forgot she was just the housekeeper, she got her feelings hurt.

She went back to the kitchen and began to prepare dinner. Out of the corner of her eye she could see their heads bent toward each other as they talked. It was good for Matt to have different company. Sighing, she put the chickens in the oven to roast.

Mindy Sue stood and waved to Summer. "Holden said to

tell you he'd be late and you're not to worry about his dinner. He'll pick something up."

With a plastered smiled, Summer nodded. "Thanks for letting me know."

Mindy Sue nodded and left, leaving Summer feeling cold. No wonder Holden had been gone so much lately. They were probably going to eat dinner together.

"Mindy Sue seems nice," Summer commented, wanting Matt's opinion.

Matt grinned. "She sure is. She is going to school in the fall. Holden is paying for it. I think it's great. They make a great team."

"Yes, they do." She swallowed hard and turned away, not wanting Matt to know her true feelings. She'd just have to get over it.

The front door slammed open, scaring her. Luke was a blur as he ran up the stairs. Minutes later he was right back down.

"I knew it! I knew it!" He planted himself right in front of her, his eyes full of anger.

"Knew what?" She tried to sound calm while a shiver went through her body.

"I told Holden you were a no good thief. He didn't believe me. He'll believe me now." The triumph in his expression startled her.

"I don't know what you mean."

Luke laughed a hard sarcastic laugh. "Yeah, right. Just give me back my money and get your ass off our land."

Her mouth dropped open as she stared at him. He appeared dead serious. "I didn't—"

"You did. Now pack your things and get out!"

"Wait a minute, Luke, exactly what are you talking about?" Her mind whirled, wondering what to do.

"I had money on my dresser when I left this morning.

Now it's gone. Don't think I haven't heard all about you from the kids in town. You might have Matt and Holden fooled but I'm onto you!"

"Luke, you're mistaken. I'd never steal from you. I don't have any money."

He crossed his arms in front of him. "Exactly, that's why you took money. You were the only one up there unless Matt somehow flew up the stairs."

The anger and condemnation in his eyes made up her mind. She hadn't been paid yet. Caleb's offer came to mind and even though it broke her heart, she decided that was the best course. "Go get Mark. I want him to know he's in charge out there. I'll… I'll just pack."

Luke's dark eyes flashed at her. "You'd better not take anything else that doesn't belong to you."

She glanced at Matt but his face seemed set in stone. She'd get no help from him. Her face heated in humiliation and she crossed her arms in front of her to keep herself from flying apart. She'd known from the start that this would be how it ended. Somehow she let her guard down. She walked up the stairs and sat on her bed wondering if she should wait for Holden to come home. The prickling at the back of her eyes decided for her. She refused to let them see her cry. It still amazed her how one accusation could follow her like a black cloud, a big, fat cloud of suspicion. Did someone really take Luke's money or was he just setting her up? She'd probably never know.

Soon her suitcase was filled. She didn't own a whole lot. Things never made a huge difference to her. The only thing of value that she owned was her mother's gold locket. Summer lifted the mattress up. It wasn't there. On her hands and knees she searched under the bed. She looked in every corner of the room. It was gone.

Finally, she took everything out of her suitcase,

shaking out each piece of clothing. The necklace wasn't there. Her heart plummeted and she hoped it was just misplaced. The thought that someone had taken it was too much. Luke was angry enough to want to get back at her but she wasn't about to accuse anyone without hard proof.

A few tears seeped out as she zipped up her case. She dashed them away with the heels of her hands. Taking a deep breath she descended the stairs, her head held high. She nodded to Mark who stood at the door and left. It was if she was on autopilot. Somehow, she finally found herself parked in front of the O'Malleys home.

Caleb came rushing out of the house and opened her door. He held out his hand and she took it. Tears fell freely now. Caleb pulled her close and she wrapped her arms around his waist and cried into his shoulder. She couldn't even enjoy the comfort of his arms around her. She felt too broken inside.

THE LIGHTS SHINING in his house gave Holden solace. It'd been a hellish day. Three horses had to be put down. He thought he'd be used to it by now but each one took a part of him. Why don't horse owners voluntarily give up ownership when they could no longer take care of the animals? The fact that the poor creatures were still alive amazed and grieved him. How they must have suffered.

All he wanted was a smile from Summer. He'd hardly seen her in the last few days and he hungered for the sight of her sweet face. It was late but all the lights in the house were on, it boded well that she was awake. His heart skipped a beat with hope.

He knew something was wrong the moment he opened

the door and all four brothers were sitting up straight, staring at him. "Okay, out with it."

"Summer left," John said his voice full of sadness.

"Good thing too. She should have been out of here days ago," Luke spat out.

"Summer's gone? What the hell happened?"

"She stole my money," Luke said, heatedly.

"So you say," Mark said shaking his head.

"All I know is Luke says his money is gone," Matt told him.

Holden put his hands up. "Now hold up. Summer took your money and left? Are you sure she won't be back? Maybe she just borrowed it. I'm sure there's some rational explanation."

Luke scowled at him. "Yes there is. She's a thief and I told her to get out."

Holden wasn't sure what to think. "So, your money was missing and you told her to leave?"

Luke nodded. "I told her to get her ass off our property. She packed and left. Good riddance."

"How much money are we talking about?" Holden couldn't wrap his mind around the whole damn thing.

"Does it matter?" Luke challenged.

"Every detail matters. Matt, what happened?"

"Mindy Sue came over and dropped off some magazines. She left and Summer was in the kitchen making dinner when Luke came storming in and ran upstairs. He came thundering back down accusing Summer of stealing his money and fired her. She looked pretty shaken and insisted that she didn't take his money. Luke screamed at her and she went upstairs and came down with her suitcase. She told Mark he was in charge until you got back, then she got in her car and left."

John jumped out of his chair. "She was all but crying and it's all Luke's fault."

Luke jumped up and faced John, squaring off. "Why you—"

Holden stepped between them. "Hold it right there. First of all, we don't fight. Second, I do all the hiring and firing. How much money and where did you see it last?"

"Twenty bucks and it was on my dresser this morning. I remembered what was said about her being a thief so I ran home to make sure it was still there." Luke held his ground.

Holden's shoulders slumped. "Oh hell, I took the money, Luke. Damn, I should have left you a note. I didn't have any cash on me and I wanted Mindy Sue to get some magazines for Matt."

Luke stood there studying the floor, shuffling his foot now and again. He didn't say a thing. Holden was hoping for an admission that he'd been wrong. John stepped toward Holden his eyes full of hope. "Can you go get her?"

Holden wished for all their sakes he could smile and say yes. "It's not that easy, John. I don't know where she went for starters. Truthfully, I don't even know if she'd even come back here. Being accused of something you didn't do is powerful. All of you know it."

John's eyes grew damp as he laid his head on Holden's middle, wrapping his arms around his waist. "I really like her."

"I know, kiddo." Holden held John's small body to him. They'd all suffered too many hardships of late. John wasn't usually a crier and each sob went straight to Holden's heart. Holden sighed. "I suppose I could go find her. It'll have to be tomorrow."

John took a step back and wiped his eyes with his sleeve. He nodded glumly. "First light."

Holden gave him what he hoped was a reassuring smile.

"First light. Now time to hit the hay." He watched as all except Matt climbed the stairs, his heart heavy.

"I should have done something," Matt lamented. "I just let her leave."

Holden sat in the chair next to him. "Listen, Matt, we are all responsible for each other but we can't be responsible for each other's actions. Do you understand what I'm trying to say?"

"We look out for each other but we can't control what the others do?"

Holden smiled and patted Matt on the shoulder. "I do believe you are no longer a boy after all."

Matt's grin was rewarding. "What do you think I've been sayin'?"

"Goodnight." His steps were heavy as he walked to his bedroom and weariness settled over him. A long couple of days and now all this. He stripped down and slipped into Matt's bed. There was no way he was sleeping in his own bed. The scent of Summer would give him no peace. He wasn't too worried about her. He knew she fled to Caleb's, despite what he told the boys. He just hoped that Caleb really did think of her as a sister.

He understood why she left. It just hurt that she didn't come straight to him. Ever since Summer came into his life, she had turned his world upside down. He'd sworn off women and here he was yearning for her to come back. He hoped he'd be able to talk her into coming home. Hadn't she used that word "home"? Pain lanced his heart as he realized how much Luke's accusation must have hurt her. To be accused once again of something she didn't do probably devastated her. All she'd given to his family, the kindness, the understanding, and she was ordered to leave. He was more unsure than ever that she'd even talk to him, let alone come back.

Luke had his issues too and Holden could understand his lack of trust for females, but hadn't she proven herself? Luke had seemed angry these last few days and now he was kicking himself for not finding out why.

He rolled onto his back and stared at the ceiling. Had it only been a little over a week since Summer entered his life? She evoked such emotion from him, passion, yearning, and protectiveness. No one had ever made him feel the way she did, no one.

He hoped that tomorrow would be a good day for all of them.

———

SUMMER LAY in bed reliving her day. How had everything gone so horribly wrong? If she had seen it coming it wouldn't have hurt as much. She told the truth about her past and everyone seemed fine with it. She wiped away a tear. Everyone but Luke.

She'd poured her heart out to Caleb who kindly and patiently listened and offered her a place to stay. She knew she couldn't stay long though. They couldn't afford to pay her and she couldn't afford to work for room and board. She needed escape money.

The loss of her necklace pained her. How could it have gone missing? The locket meant more to her than anything else. It had her parents' picture in it. She could remember her mother wearing it every day and now it was gone.

Life had certainly slammed her to the ground the last three months. She kept getting back up to fight but maybe enough was enough. What if she didn't have any fight left? Her best bet was to get out of town, but the only way she could do that was to ask for Holden to pay her.

The pain of being accused of something she didn't do was

all encompassing, pushing her down again and again. She was raised to own up to her mistakes, apologize and hope the apology was accepted. You can't apologize for something you didn't do, and the anger builds until finally it becomes too draining.

She deserved to be in a place where her character wasn't in question. Summer laughed to herself. People had often told her that she was too nice. It was her nature and that she couldn't change. Sleep came hard but she was grateful that she had a place to lay her head.

SUMMER AWOKE to the smell of coffee and quickly slid out of bed. She had wanted to make breakfast for Colt and Caleb. She dressed quickly, brushed her teeth, ran a comb quickly through her hair and bounded into the kitchen.

Caleb sat at the big wooden farm table, holding a cup of coffee and grinning at her. "Morning, Summer."

His grin was always infectious and she found herself smiling in return. "I hadn't planned to sleep so late. I want to earn my keep."

"I have a feeling you won't be here long enough."

"What's that supposed to mean? I can't stay? I'll only be here a few days."

"Whoa, slow down." The wooden chair creaked as he stood up. He quickly poured a new cup of coffee and handed it to her. "You can stay as long as you like. I just meant that the O'Leary clan will be here for you in a bit."

Her eyes widened. "Caleb, what are you talking about?"

Caleb laughed. "I just got a secret call from John. He must have been standing in the closet or something. He is coming to bring you home and so are his brothers."

Stunned she sat down and stared at Caleb, searching his brown eyes for some sign of a joke. He was serious. "Why?"

"All I know is John said that Luke is a great big ass."

She didn't know whether to laugh or cry. "I don't think I can go back there."

Caleb reached over and took her small hand in his. "It's up to you. My only advice is to listen to what they have to say.

Summer nodded, Caleb taking her hand in his gave her much needed strength. "It's just that I feel as though I've been kicked around a lot lately."

Caleb squeezed her hand. "Darlin' you have every reason to hold you head up high. I hear them driving up now."

Her stomach did flips as apprehension filled her. Looking out the front window, she saw Colt walk out of the barn to greet the O'Learys. "I can't do this." She let go of Caleb's hand and started to walk toward the bedroom. Caleb blocked her path.

"Summer, don't run from this. You'll always wonder what they had to say to you."

She lifted her head and locked gazes with Caleb and was surprised when he hauled her against him for a quick hug. Perhaps it wasn't quick enough. The door opened and she heard a gasp. She took a step back and turned. Holden stood there with his brothers behind him. She saw his disgruntled expression but that didn't matter. Matt had accompanied them. She quickly flew to Matt's side and helped him into a chair, giving Holden the look of the devil.

"Matt, you shouldn't be on your feet."

He gave her a lopsided grin. "I'm the extra insurance."

She crossed her arms in front of her and stared at Holden. "Insurance?"

Holden's face turned red. He was just about to speak when John scooted in front of him.

"You know insurance in case you said no. Matt would groan in pain and you'd have to come back home." His face was so earnest that Summer's heart softened.

"Is that so? I was under the impression that I was fired." She shot Holden a quick look. He looked like he was about to speak again but John came running toward her, almost knocking her to the ground.

"You have to come back. Please, Summer?" His arms tightened around her waist.

Holden cleared his throat. "It was a misunderstanding and we would be obliged if you would come back."

There was a vague vulnerability in his dark eyes that made her wonder. His eyebrows rose as though he was waiting for an answer. Where was the apology? Calling something a misunderstanding was not acknowledging the wrong that was done to her.

She wavered. "I just need you to pay me for the work I've already done and I'll be out of everyone's hair. It's for the best." Her heart squeezed painfully but it was the right thing to do. She couldn't live with them anymore.

Holden's face hardened and John let her go. Matt looked away as did Mark. Luke stepped forward.

"It was my fault, Summer. I blamed you and it was Holden who took my money. I didn't even ask you if you knew anything about it. I just accused you. I'm sorry."

The pleading expression on his face melted her. She wasn't Luke's favorite person and it probably was hard for him to apologize. Damn, she wanted to go with them but was it wise?

"Boys get back into the trucks. Be careful with Matt. I want to talk to Summer for a moment." Holden shot Caleb a glance. "Could you give us a minute?"

She watched as each sullen boy left. Caleb squeezed her shoulder on his way out. What she didn't do was look at

Holden. He had too much power over her emotions. The silence between them was so awkward she finally glanced up at him.

He studied her and sighed. "I know I can't change your mind. It must have been horrifying to be accused again and I'm sorrier than you will ever know. You don't deserve such treatment by anyone. I'll just say this, I need you and the boys need you. Home isn't the same without you there. I guess it sounds stupid, we've only known you a short time but we've become attached to you."

She smiled sadly. "You're right, it was horrifying and heartbreaking. I think I'm getting too attached your family. I went through hell yesterday and to tell you the truth I just don't know how many times I can keep getting up and dusting myself off."

Holden closed the distance between them and grabbed her up into a hug. He kissed her temple and whispered, "I'm sorry."

Summer bit her lip to keep from crying. She already soaked one man's shirt in the last twenty-four hours. She wasn't planning to do it again. She could feel him shiver against her. He cared. She nodded against his chest.

Holden quickly kissed her cheek and let her go. "Get packed. I'll let the guys know." He started for the door but stopped and turned, staring at her. "Thank you."

She smiled and watched him fly out the door. She hoped she was doing the right thing. As if she even had inkling what was right anymore. It had been a long time since someone had apologized; she had to give Luke credit for that. Her necklace was still missing but she had a feeling it would turn up soon.

CHAPTER SIX

*S*he stood at the top of the stairs. Her clothes were all put away and her nerves were getting the better of her. Reluctantly, she slowly walked down the stairs. Every eye was upon her, gauging her, and she wanted to hide. She wasn't quite sure how to act or how to proceed. The awkwardness weighed heavily. She gave them all a brief smile and continued to the kitchen. The coffee was already made, so she poured herself a cup and decided to make breakfast. It would keep her busy.

"We already ate." John's voice directly behind her startled her.

She turned. "Where are the dirty dishes?"

Everyone snickered and she didn't know what to think. Then she noticed everyone but Luke was laughing. He met her gaze for a brief second then looked at the floor. Her heart opened to him. He really was just a boy.

She put her coffee down and walked to Luke, who still studied the floor. "You did the dishes didn't you?" she asked softly.

Luke finally raised his head and she could see sheen of tears in his eyes. "It was nothing."

She wished she could pull him into her arms and hug him, but he'd never allow that. Instead she smiled. "Thank you."

He nodded and looked away, apparently uncomfortable with the whole situation. She knew how he felt. All of his brothers stared intently.

"Hey, don't you guys have a ranch to run or something?" She winked at John.

John puffed up his chest. "We sure do."

She smiled as they all filed out until it was just her and Matt. Then her smile faded.

"Hard few days," he commented.

Summer nodded. "You're not kidding."

"Holden shouldn't have borrowed Luke's money without telling him. He gave the money to Mindy Sue to buy me magazines."

Mindy Sue again, it figured. "Well I'm glad it's all sorted out and you have something to read. I have laundry to do. I'll check on you in a few. Need anything before I go?"

Matt stared at her and shook his head. He could see right through her, she could tell. Somehow he was wiser than his years sometimes.

Gathering the dirty laundry didn't take long. She wondered if she truly could just act as though nothing had happened, but she didn't know of any other way to act. Loneliness settled over once again. She'd never missed her mom and dad as much as these past few months. It'd been cathartic to talk to Caleb but it wasn't the same. She longed for something solid, something real. Was true love an illusion? She swore she'd never allow any man hurt her and here she was, feeling as though her heart was bleeding.

She whole heartedly wished for inner peace. It was too

exhausting trying to act as though everything was fine. Nothing was fine. Would she forever have a cloud of suspicion over her? Why couldn't they see that she'd been beaten too? So far they hadn't been bothered by her nightmares but it was becoming harder to keep them at bay.

It wore on her, trying to be the strong one. She wanted Brent caught and she wanted her good name back. Her plastered smiles ate at her soul. She couldn't keep smiling, not when her world was falling apart. Holden would have been her greatest love in another place, in another time, but not this one.

What would happen when school started in the fall? Would Mark, Luke and John be made to pay for her perceived mistakes? She'd wither if that happened. They were great boys and deserved better than that. No matter how many times she told herself that she was innocent, in the end it only mattered what others thought.

"Honey, you up there?" Holden yelled.

She wasn't anyone's "honey" but there was no sense in saying so now. She left the laundry basket and stood at the top of the stairs gazing down at Holden. His beautiful lips curved into a sexy grin and his chocolate eyes beckoned her. Before she knew it she was standing right in front of him, on the last step, eye level with him. Her breath caught. He smelled of horses and sweat but she didn't care. To her everything about him was sexy. Everything.

He peered into her eyes holding her to that spot. He seemed to like what he saw and it gladdened her heart. It shouldn't but it did. There could only be one outcome between them and someone was going to get hurt. She hoped she could get through it.

He grabbed her hand and tugged her down the last step. His hard body pressed against hers. He was unlike anyone she'd ever known. His shoulders were broad and she knew he had the weight of raising his brothers on them, yet he took her problems on too. He made her feel small and dainty and protected.

"Come on, I want you to meet Yukon."

"I've already met that darn horse. He didn't take a liking to me."

Holden pulled her along. "You just didn't have the right introduction. He's practically a puppy now."

She laughed. "Hey, Matt, what do you think?"

Matt chuckled. "As long as you don't get too close. Take a ten foot pole so you'll know how close is close enough."

She hoped he was kidding. "I really don't know…"

"Come on woman. You grew up on a ranch."

She shifted her weight until he stopped. "I am not getting on that that beast of a horse."

Holden turned and grabbed her waist. He lifted her up until she was draped over his shoulder. "No one said you had to ride him. I just want you to meet him."

Under extreme protest, Summer was carried to the corral. The audacity of that man. He slapped her ass when she pounded on his back. Holden put her down and she gave him her best dirty look.

Holden's laugh was loud and deep. "You don't fool me with that look. Besides you need practice. Luke is much better at mean looks."

To her dismay, laughter bubbled up inside of her. There was no way to remove the smile on her face. "What am I going to do with you?"

His eyebrows rose. "Do you want a list or should we just wing it?" His was voice suggestive.

"I didn't say it that way."

Holden winked. "So you say."

The realization that he was flirting with her hit her hard.

She stared at him, her mouth agape, while he gave her an incredibly sexy grin. "So, where is Yukon?"

"Yukon who?"

Summer punched him in the arm. His arms were solid muscle. He didn't even flinch and it was her best punch.

"Shh. Yukon is coming and I don't want him to think badly of you."

Summer glanced at him, shook her head and glanced toward the barn. Sure enough, Mark was leading Yukon out. The stallion didn't seem so dangerous on a lead rope. Still her muscles tightened.

Holden patted her rear. "Relax."

Talk about keeping her off balance! Scooting away, she kept her gaze on Yukon. She wasn't sure that she liked this touchy feely Holden. What about Mindy Sue? Being suspicious sucked. It was taking the fun out of her. Holden's playfulness was a reminder that she hadn't had real fun in a very long time.

Once Yukon was in the corral, Holden whistled. The big bay stallion trotted right over to him. The quarter horse stood bigger than life. His well-muscled legs were black covered by white markings while his muzzle, mane and tail, and the tips of his ears were black.

"Up close he's massive." Yukon awed her.

Holden nodded. "Don't worry, honey, I'll take care of you."

She opened her mouth to reply.

"Now be calm. Yukon likes calm."

Summer stood still, watching Holden talk to Yukon. Yukon allowed Holden close enough to talk into his ear. She could hardly believe that this was the same horse she ran in terror from. It was a joy to watch them. Holden was in his element. There was no wonder at all why he was a vet. He really was an exceptional man.

"Take a picture it lasts longer."

Summer turned to see John sticking his tongue out at her. "What?"

"Goo goo eyes and it wasn't Yukon you were looking at either." His bright, teasing smile made her blush.

Glancing at Holden, her blush deepened at his knowing smile. "So, are you going to introduce me to Yukon or what?"

Holden held out his hand to her and when she clasped it, he drew her slowly to his side. "Yukon, this is my filly, Summer."

Summer pretended that she didn't hear him. "Hello, Yukon."

Yukon stared at her for a while then with a fleeting glance at Holden, he trotted off to the far side of the corral. Holden squeezed her hand. "I think he likes you." He gasped as Summer elbowed him in the ribs.

"I'm sure he has a thing for fillies."

Holden laughed. "It's a male thing, you wouldn't understand."

Shaking her head, she realized that there was no winning.

"Come on I'll take you on a tour of the barn. I have more horses." His phone buzzed, and he answered it. "I'll be right there, Mindy Sue."

He looked down at Summer. "I'm sorry the tour will have to wait."

"I understand. A horse?"

"No, a couple of dogs got into a fight. I need to stitch them up." He surprised her with a kiss on the cheek before he left.

Summer wondered what the heck was going on. She thought he didn't like her and now, he was too affectionate and she felt conflicted. Part of her soaked up the attention and the other part called her a fool. She walked to the house making a mental list of things that needed to be done, trying to get it off her mind.

The phone was ringing when she walked in and Matt was trying to stand. She flew across the room and grabbed the phone. "Hello?"

"So, it's true. You are there."

"Brent? You have some nerve calling me. Where have you been? They think I was in on it."

"Don't worry so much, Summer. You are still very much a part of my plans."

"I'm hanging up and I never want you to call me again."

"Wait! I just want to finish what I started."

"What the hell are you talking about?" she demanded.

"I got interrupted the last time I saw you. Think about it."

He hung up and Summer stared at the phone, her heart beating a loud tattoo. Her body began to shake and tears filled her eyes. What did he mean? Oh God, she knew exactly what he meant. That's why she was naked but not…

"Summer?" Matt's voice was filled with concern. "Summer, you're pale. You better sit before you faint."

"What?" A blanket of fog surrounded her. Fear pulsed through her body. Sit down, Matt said to sit. She sat on a wooden kitchen chair. How? Why? Finish?

"We should call the police. It was that Brent guy wasn't it?"

"No. No police. They never believe a word I say."

"Maybe they can trace the call, Summer."

"No. I have to vacuum upstairs. You'll be okay for a while?"

"Of course but I really think—"

"Matt, could we talk about this later? If I have to talk to the sheriff again, I'll have a meltdown."

Doubt clouded his face. "For now."

Summer nodded. "Thanks." Climbing the stairs she

wished she could run and hide, but where? Brent murdered Paul. If she talked to the sheriff he'd probably just throw her in jail. If she didn't—oh hell, either way she was toast. All she'd accomplished was bringing danger to the O'Learys.

Calling Holden wasn't an option. She couldn't drag the O'Malleys into this either. She turned on the vacuum and tears rolled down her face. She had to keep busy or go crazy, but how was she going to keep her mind occupied? Why would Brent contact her? Nothing made sense. She'd ask Holden for her money and take off. Oh hell, she just got back.

She vacuumed until her strength gave out. It was an empty feeling, being on your own. Turning the vacuum off she heard Holden clearing his throat behind her. She must have been vacuuming much longer than she thought. Summer closed her eyes and took a deep breath. Slowly she let it out and opened her eyes. She turned and the concerned expression on Holden's face was her undoing. She ran into his open arms and held on for dear life.

"Matt told me as much as he knew." He tightened the hug, holding her against him.

He felt so safe and she wished that staying in his arms was an option. Her body shook and she knew he could feel it. Finally, she pulled away and stared at him.

"I can tell that you have leaving on your mind. Forget about it. I want you here."

"He's a murderer. I can't stay. He could harm your family."

"That's true. I'm calling the sheriff and before you object, I want you to know I will be right there with you. Honey, he needs to know."

He looked so sincere. Her first instinct was to say no, but maybe the sheriff could help keep Holden's family safe. "Okay." She nodded reluctantly.

Holden gave her an encouraging smile and took her small

shaking hand into his big firm one. "Come on. We have a phone call to make."

THE WARINESS on Summer's face went right to Holden's heart. He promised himself no more women until the boys were all grown up. Summer snuck right past his barriers and he had a feeling she wasn't all happy about it either.

At first he thought it was purely sexual but now his heart was vested. He couldn't push his feelings away any longer. He wanted her with a ferocity that he'd never felt before. He wanted the whole package including her love.

By the way her body stiffened, he knew that Sheriff Brown had arrived. She wanted to flee; he could see it in her eyes. He went to her and hugged her. The boys were on the porch and they let the sheriff in.

Holden went and shook hands with him. "Thank you for coming out here."

Sheriff Brown nodded and his eyes zeroed in on Summer. "So, I was right all along. He did contact you."

Summer gasped and her hand went to her throat. "He did contact me, today."

"Summer, give it up. Just tell me where your boyfriend is."

Holden closed the distance between himself and Summer. He stood at her side and stared the sheriff down. "Brent called here, yes. It was the first time."

"Well, thank you for telling me. I'll file a report." He turned to leave.

"Where are you going? Summer is scared out of her mind and that's all you have to say?"

Sheriff Brown turned to them and smiled. "Now this is an —what do you call it? An analogy for you. Lay down with dogs and you're bound to get fleas."

"He threatened her. For the love of God, what is wrong with you?"

"Listen Holden, you seem like a nice guy and you have your brothers to worry about. Don't burden yourself with this one. She lies and steals and is an accomplice to murder. I can't make the charges stick yet, but I will. Can't you see she's just covering her tracks by telling me about the call? Brent probably calls here all the time and you just don't know it."

Holden felt gut kicked. "No extra protection?"

The sheriff laughed. "You think about those fleas, they bite." He was still laughing as he went out the door.

"Damn it!" Holden took a step toward the door. Summer's hand on his arm stopped him.

"Please, Holden, don't make it worse. It'll be all over town by tomorrow. I knew he wouldn't believe me but I didn't expect him to laugh either."

John ran into the house straight at Summer. "I'll protect you!"

His little earnest face brought tears to her eyes. "I know you will." She glanced up and exchanged gazes with Holden. His plea for her to stay was evident in his eyes.

Blinking back tears, she kissed the top of John's head. She almost laughed when he wiped it away. He made her heart smile.

"I just don't want anything to happen to any of you because of me."

Mark stood tall. "We're the O'Learys and we take care of ourselves."

Holden grinned. "That we do."

Summer glanced at Luke. His opinion mattered. "I'll put a bullet in anyone that tries to hurt you." His voice was hard and serious.

"Okay, guys no bullets," she said. They weren't nodding in agreement.

"Unless absolutely necessary," Holden added.

Bullets? What in world? "Holden, can I talk to you alone for a minute?" She headed for the door, hoping he'd follow.

As soon as the door closed, she whirled around to face him. "Why are we talking about bullets? I don't want one hair on those boys heads hurt. Guns are not the answer. How many guns do you have? They're locked up right?"

Holden held both hands up in surrender. "Whoa, Summer. Yes we have guns. Yes they are in several gun safes."

"Several?"

"Listen, you grew up around here, certainly you know the dangers that are out there. There are plenty of wild animals, etcetera. We need our rifles. There is a safe in my closet, one in the barn, and one behind a hidden panel in the great room. They have keypad locks and we all know the combination."

"You're a militia."

"Not quite. We only use them for protection. We've never had to pull a gun on anyone nor do we ever expect to. They just wanted you to feel safe."

Summer sighed as she stared into his brown eyes. "You'll talk to them? I don't want them with guns waiting for Brent to show up."

Holden stepped forward and brushed her cheek with the back of his hand. He tucked a stray hair behind her ear and kissed her cheek. "Don't worry."

She nodded but knew that there was no way to keep from worrying. Life had led her to many places, this being the best. But it was true, she was trouble.

"I'm sorry I didn't listen to you about the sheriff." He enfolded her in his strong arms.

It felt so good to be so close. He smelled of leather and soap. Summer burrowed against him, cherishing the comfort. She could really fall for him if she wasn't careful. Her heart thumped in her chest. Hell, it was too late for caution. Turning her head she placed her ear over his chest and smiled. Out of the corner of her eye she saw John and Luke at the window sticking their tongues out at her. "We'd better go in. We have an audience."

Holden was slow to let her go. "I'm a package deal you know."

Pulling back, she lifted her gaze to meet his dark eyes. "I know and I like the package."

"If we didn't have two—oh make that three—voyeurs, I'd kiss you senseless," he said, his voice husky with promises.

Holden's phone rang and once again he had an emergency to attend to. "A horse that's been standing in wet mud for days. He can barely walk. It's a damn shame."

"Go, rescue the horse. I'll be here when you get home."

The smile she got in response curled her toes. She watched him drive off feeling like a school girl again. She wondered what type of teasing she was in for when she went back inside.

No teasing, just goofy smiles, and Luke asked to talk to her upstairs.

He led her to his bedroom and reached under his mattress. He had a pained expression on his face as he held out her locket. "I'm sorry."

Summer couldn't stay mad. He seemed lost and sorry. "Thank you. I'm glad to have it back." She opened the locket. "They are my parents. They died a few years back and I was heartbroken when I couldn't find it."

"I thought you stole my money."

"I know you did, Luke, but stealing to get back at someone is wrong. You know that don't you?"

Luke nodded glumly. "It's just with all the shit that went down in Texas all because of some skirt, I thought you were the same."

More hints to a secret Texas past. She longed to know

what happened but it wasn't her place to ask. "Thank you for giving it back to me."

Luke glanced at the floor avoiding her gaze. So, you're not mad?"

"No, we're good."

Luke smiled, and then raced past her and down the stairs.

Summer held the precious locket to her heart. She missed her parents.

CHAPTER SEVEN

*H*olden shook Jonas' hand. Out of all the men, Jonas was the biggest and strongest. "I don't know if we'd have gotten her on and off the trailer without you, Jonas."

"Poor, old Jinky. I didn't even hear of Miss Calvin's passing or I would have been out here to check on the mare."

"She'd been stuck in that mud for some time. Look how thin she is." Holden shook his head in disgust.

They both leaned on the stall gate in Jonas' barn. "I'll try to get her to eat," Jonas assured him.

"I know you will. I'm impressed with your dedication. There aren't enough hours in the day for me to give every horse my full attention and raising my brothers…"

"Must be tough. I have plenty of time."

"Not married?"

"No. I haven't found a lady yet. I was in the Army. I'm a bit battle scarred."

Holden could see the pain in the big, brown haired, amber eyed man. "It's hard to find the right one for sure."

"Don't you have that pretty Summer working for you?"

"Yes." Holden hesitated, waiting in dread for Jonas to tell him about the murder.

"Hold on to that one. She's got a heart as big as Montana. She was always as sweet as sugar. Damn thing with the sheriff and old lady Rain spreading nasty rumors about her. Tell her I said hi and to keep her chin up. There are plenty of people here about that believe her."

Holden nodded in relief. "I'll tell her. See you in the morning. If anything comes up call."

"Will do."

It had been a long rescue. He'd have to get records of every animal in the county and keep track of owner deaths. Jinky didn't look good at all. She had Equine Scratches, an infection of the lower leg. Her skin had become crusted, scabby and thickened. It was a severe case. Her skin oozed and her lower legs swelled. If left untreated the horse would become lame. That was his biggest fear. Hopefully, Jonas could get her to eat. The next few days would be crucial. He rubbed the back of his neck. The stiffness was fierce. He was anxious to see Summer; he needed to know that she was still there.

Life was constantly changing. He wished he could take Summer's pain away. It was corny but she really was like a summer's day. She brought sunshine and warmth into his life. Somehow he didn't feel as tired getting into his truck. He laughed at himself and pushed down on the accelerator pedal to get home faster.

The house came into view and he sighed. Parking his truck, he took a deep breath. He didn't want to seem too eager to see her. She shied away at times if he gave her too much attention.

Holden frowned, spotting Luke sitting on the porch steps. "What's up Luke?"

"I did something I'm not proud of and I wanted to be the one to tell you." Luke kept his gaze on his boots.

Holden sat down next to his brother. "Go ahead, I'm listening."

"I stole Summer's necklace when I thought she stole my money." He glanced up at Holden as though he was trying to gauge his reaction.

"Did you give it back?"

Luke nodded.

"Did you apologize?"

Luke nodded again, still staring intently.

Holden nodded. "It's not good that you took the necklace, but it is good that you gave it back. It takes a real man to apologize for his actions. I'm assuming Summer accepted your apology?"

"Yes, she did. I am sorry."

Holden stood and ruffled Luke's hair. "I know you are. Glad you two are square." He walked into the house. Luke was growing up so fast. They all were.

Summer was making tea in the kitchen. Holden watched her for a moment. She looked so fresh and pretty in her white shorts and pink t-shirt. He admired her curvy figure. Her honey blond hair was in a French braid and he wished he had the right to undo it and run his fingers through her silky locks.

She turned and smiled. Suddenly he didn't feel as weary. "Any dinner left?"

"Of course. I'd never let you go hungry. Have a seat and I'll get your plate."

"Thank you. I'm grateful that there's food left. My brothers eat tons." He pulled back the wooden chair and sat down.

"Oh, I'm on to them. I make a plate for you first." She chuckled as she put a heaping plate before him.

"I appreciate it. There have been many nights I've had cold food out of a can."

"You look tired." Summer sat in the chair across from him, her eyes full of compassion.

"It was a long one. Did you know Miss Calvin?"

"Yes, she was a fine woman. Too bad about her passing."

"Her horse, Jinky, was still in a pen out back, standing in deep mud."

"Oh no! Were you able to help her?"

"The hardest part was getting her onto the trailer. Her feet are so tender she could hardly walk. Jonas and I had to lift her hooves one by one to get her walking and onto the trailer. Getting her back off and into a fresh stall was just as hard. Thank God, Jonas is a big guy."

Summer nodded. "Jonas is a sweetheart. I'm so sorry about Jinky. Is she lame?"

"We'll know in a day or two. I'm going out there in the morning. Doesn't anyone check the barns for animals when a person dies?"

"Truthfully, I never gave it much thought. I thought there was an agency that did all that." She gazed at him with concern.

It had been a long while since someone was concerned about just him. Usually he was the one that worried. It felt nice to have Summer here to share his day. Suddenly she blushed and averted her eyes. She must have realized she was staring at him.

"Jonas thinks the world of you, Summer. He told me that most of the folks are in your corner. It's a few nasty ones that believe the sheriff."

"Really? Thank you for telling me. Jonas is one of a kind." Her brief smile was sad.

"He said he was battle scarred?"

Summer nodded. "We weren't sure he'd make it when he came home. Shrapnel I believe. He won't talk about it and I never wanted to make him uncomfortable. He has a slight limp but to him it's a huge limp. He refuses to believe otherwise."

"So, you two are good friends?" Somehow he hoped not, he wanted her for himself.

"I suppose. He'd come into the bar and grill now and then. Always sat at the bar. I grew up here, Holden. Carlston really is a great place. Sure we have the gossips but there have been plenty of people that have helped me at one time or another."

"Yet, you were leaving town if you didn't get the job here."

Summer nodded and sighed. "The sheriff harassed anyone that was offering to take me in."

"That man needs an attitude adjustment."

"I'll help," Luke volunteered, walking toward them.

"That's very noble, Luke, but I think it's best to just stay out of Sheriff Brown's way." Summer smiled at Luke. Her affection for him glowing in her blue eyes.

Luke smiled and Holden bet it was being called noble that did it. "Well if you guys will check on Matt before you go to bed I'd appreciate it. I need my beauty sleep."

"Sure, Summer. Good night." Holden watched her climb the stairs. Her legs were long and her rear swayed enticingly. He'd bide his time, for now but hell, he wanted her.

HEADING UP TO HER ROOM, Summer didn't quite know what to think as far as Holden was concerned. The glint in his eyes pleased her. Perhaps a little too much. It was a relief Jonas and many of the town's people didn't blame her for Paul's death, but she was still scared out of her wits. Brent meant what he said and he'd be coming for her. Maybe she should have told Holden but she was half afraid that Holden would go after Brent and get hurt.

She quickly put her nightgown on and shut off the light. She dragged the wooden chair to the window that over-looked the front of the house. Drawing the heavy curtain aside, she stared out into the darkness watching, waiting, and worrying.

She never felt the way she felt about Holden before. He was in her heart and it was going to hurt when it was all over. Would it be better to stay guarded with him or would she regret never making love with him? He made her whole body sing and she desperately wanted to just wrap her whole self around him. He'd awakened a whole side of her she wasn't familiar with. Of course she'd had sex before but she instinctively knew that it would be so different with Holden. Her nipples tightened and she crossed her arms over them, her whole being wistful.

Sleep didn't even enter her mind as she stared out the window. Brent was someone she thought she knew, but he had fooled her. She'd thought they shared a mutual affection when they broke up. There were no hard feelings, their schedules didn't mesh. But, he used her and like a fool, she didn't even know.

How could she not have seen the violence in him? There must have been some signs that she missed. What the signs were, she had no idea. He mentioned he'd been interrupted, by whom? Did he plan to rape her or was murder in his plans too? Chills racked her body.

She couldn't sit still any longer, so she paced back and forth, mentally kicking herself for being so stupid. Although she appreciated that the O'Learys wanted to protect her, they hadn't seen the carnage Brent left. Paul's murder had been particularly brutal. Sheriff Brown made sure she saw it up close before she was taken to the hospital. What an ass.

A knock on her door, staunched her thoughts. Opening it, there stood Holden, bare-chested. Her mouth dropped open as she stared. She'd never seen so many well developed muscles on a man before. His shoulders seemed to take up the whole width of the doorframe. A light sprinkling of dark hair covered his chest tapering down to a fine line that disappeared under his jeans. Realizing she was staring, she immediately glanced up. Her face grew warm at his knowing grin. His damn, sexy grin of his was going to get her in trouble.

"I saw your shadow walking back and forth under the door. Is that what you wear to bed? What if one of the boys needed you in the middle of the night?"

"I-I have a robe. I was just distracted is all." Damn, she was wearing her very sheer rose colored nightgown. "I'll get it. Is one of the boys sick?"

Before she could turn, she found herself in Holden's arms, plastered against his rock hard body. Her nipples tightened to the point of hurting. He lowered his head and swept in for a kiss. It was a bold demanding kiss that had her aching even more. She instantly put her arms around his neck, pulling his head down, intensifying the richness of the kiss. Instantly, she opened for him and his tongue darted inside, dancing with hers. Her breathing became labored as she ran her fingers through his thick, brown hair. Her moans sounded loud in the quiet room.

Holden picked her up without breaking the kiss. He held her rear in his big hands as she wrapped her legs around his tapered waist. He used his foot to close the door behind him. He broke the kiss and pulled one strap of her gown down her arm with his teeth, and then he slowly did the other. The top part pooled around her waist. He stared at her breasts and she felt a jolt inside of her. He laid her on the bed and feasted on her breasts. Taking one nipple in his warm mouth, he sucked on it, then the other. He rolled her nipples between his fingers.

A wildness enveloped her. She wasn't usually aggressive in bed but she was in need. It only took her seconds to get his belt off and his fly undone. She felt cold when he released her to remove his Wranglers. But the cold was well worth it. He was so hard and big that her breath caught in her throat. He slipped the rest of her gown off and stepped back staring at her. The look of admiration in his eyes made her feel beautiful. Opening her arms she invited him to love her.

He kissed his way from her throat to her thighs, and his kisses were pure magic. He found the right spot and kissed her, causing her to cry out. She was ready, so ready for him and he didn't keep her waiting. The next thing she knew he was inside of her. Any doubts she had that he wouldn't fit were quickly dashed.

Summer panted as he thrust into her. Soon she matched his rhythm loving every minute of it. "Keep your beautiful eyes open. I want to see them," Holden urged, his voice low and husky.

Smiling at him, she locked her gaze with his as they continued. She felt it coming; intense pleasure had built to its full height. She cried out still staring into his dark eyes. His cry of satisfaction followed hers. He was right.I It was miraculous gazing into each other's eyes. His eyes glowed with passion and she tingled everywhere. It had been everything she imagined and more.

Holden moved and lay down next to her, taking her into his arms. "That was—well all I can say is wow."

Summer turned toward him and raised herself up on her elbow. Smiling, she kissed his cheek. "Wow is right." Snuggling against him was pure heaven. She was just about fall asleep when the bed jostled. Holden got up and put on his pants. She waited for him to look back at her but he didn't. Part of her knew he had to leave. What would his brother's think if they found him in her room? Part of her felt let down. It was as if he was sneaking out on her. As she slowly fell asleep she decided to just hang on to the wow.

CHAPTER EIGHT

 he next few days were a rollercoaster of emotion for Summer. She sat on the front porch drinking some evening coffee, watching the magnificent sunset. The colors splashed across the mountains in an array of pinks and purples brought a smile to her lips. It gave her the first sense of peace since she slept with Holden three nights ago.

She sipped her coffee and her smile turned sad. He'd hardly looked at her, and it hurt to her very core. What she thought was making love, was just sex to him. He never acknowledged it and his easy affection toward her had ceased. He'd stolen the wow from her. Her heart ached and she had no one to blame but herself. She'd had her doubts and like a fool she dismissed them. She and Holden were obviously not on the same page.

Her heart constricted. She never cared about a man this much before and the pain was almost too much. Maybe she was too naïve—too stupid was more like it. How could she have imagined a man like Holden would want to be with her? She was a different person from before the beating Brent gave her. She used to be outgoing and more confident. Now she didn't feel confident at all. Damaged goods is what her mother would have said. Just good enough for a roll in the hay but never good enough to marry. She'd known women like that, many came into the bar. They all were a bit lost and that was how she felt.

The slam of the front door jarred her from her musings. "Hi Mark. Come enjoy the sunset with me."

Mark sat in the chair next to her. "Looks nice all right." He hesitated as though he was trying to think of conversation to make.

"Is something bothering you, Mark?"

"I was going to ask you that same question." Mark's face turned red.

Summer glanced away from him so he wouldn't see the lies in her eyes. "I'm fine. Everything seems to be going well around here. Matt is feeling better."

"But you're not happy."

Summer bit her bottom lip. "I'm just moody sometimes is all. Really, don't pay attention to me when I get like this."

Mark touched her arm. "Are you sure? You haven't gotten any more calls from the creep have you?"

Relief washed over her. "No calls at all." She turned toward him and plastered a smile on her face. "It's been nice and quiet."

Mark nodded. "Sometimes it seems that way when Holden is gone so much."

"He has been busy of late."

"He's teaching Mindy Sue some new system or something. Once they get it all figured out I'm sure he'll be home more."

Fake smiles were becoming her specialty. "It shouldn't be too much longer." She didn't want Mark to know that she didn't know Holden was spending his time with Mindy Sue.

She sat with Mark in silence until she finished her coffee. "I'm heading in."

Mark nodded. "Goodnight, Summer."

She waltzed by a snoozing Matt, and smiled at Luke and John who were playing a video game. Putting her cup in the sink, she wondered if Holden was with Mindy Sue tonight too. If only he was around once in awhile she'd be able to talk to him. "Goodnight," she whispered to Luke and John. "Don't stay up too late." A good night's sleep was all she wanted. All she needed.

Later that night she heard Holden's footsteps walk by her door. He didn't hesitate, just walked by. It hurt. It shouldn't have but it did. They made no promises to each other. It had been bad judgment on her part but she still craved his touch. Closing her eyes, she hoped for her cravings to go away, but opening her eyes again, she knew that would probably never happen.

THE NEXT DAY Holden sat on the top of the corral fence watching Mark and Luke work with two of their mares. They sure were good with animals. They made him proud with their knowledge. The mare Mark was trying to get saddle broke was a beautiful Palomino whose name was Links. Luke was working with a bay named Jessie. She had a sweet nature about her. Links was known to bite the other horses, but she hadn't taken a step toward Jessie this morning.

It was a hot one. Perspiration trickled down his back. He'd been spending far too much time thinking about Summer lately. Teaching Mindy Sue how to input all the animals and owners had been a bit of a chore and his distraction made it go slower than he expected. They only listed the ones they knew of. The hard part was going to be finding the rest.

Summer had been a bit chilly toward him. He didn't blame her, but his work came first. He laughed as Links tried to unseat Mark. Mark's dark hair was long under his hat and he was the picture of their father. Warmth filled his heart. Their parents would have been proud of them. John ambled out of the house and joined Holden. He climbed the fence and sat next to him, giving Holden sidelong glances.

"Okay, out with it." Holden said.

John turned toward him. "It's Summer. Are you ignoring her on purpose? Did she make you mad?"

Confused, Holden shook his head. "What makes you think that?"

"Well, the goo goo eyes are gone and so are the smiles."

Holden shook his head. "You know for such a squirt you sure know a lot." He smiled. "I hadn't realized. I guess I'd better get into the house and make some goo goo eyes at her."

John smiled brightly. "Good and I'm not a squirt."

Holden hopped down from the fence. "You're right you aren't. Thanks for the advice." He grinned, noticing John sitting taller.

Walking toward the house Holden realized that he needed a smile from Summer. There she was bending over, cleaning mud off the floor. He wanted to cup her delectable bottom in his hands. His body responded so quickly that he felt uncomfortable. Even glancing at Matt didn't squash the rising temperature inside him.

"Need some help?"

Summer straightened and turned. Her face was a rosy red and he wondered if it was because of him or maybe it was just because she had been bending over. "I've got it. Thanks though. Did you need something?" There was no warmth in her voice. In fact it sounded downright stony. He got as close as possible without actually touching her and leaned in a bit then whispered, "Yes, I need you naked and in bed."

The look in her eyes showed her doubt. "I'm busy."

"We could clean your bedroom together if you like." He grinned at her. She seemed flustered and he liked it.

"Maybe later." She started to walk away but turned back when he put his hand on her arm. "Do you mean that?" he asked holding his breath.

"No, I don't, I can't. Look, Holden, I'm not the type of woman you think I am. I have real feelings and I don't sleep around. You've made it clear that last time didn't mean anything to you. It has to mean something or it's not right. Not right for me at least."

"Oh hell," He rubbed the back of his stiff neck. "I've been busy."

"Too busy to give me the time of day? You've ignored me, Holden, and I just can't handle a casual relationship right now. It was wrong."

Dumbfounded, his mouth dropped open. "Is that what you think? I just slept with you without feeling anything for you?" He could see the answer in her sad eyes. "Honey, I'm not that man. I don't go around sleeping with women for the heck of it. Truly it has been a busy last few days and I'm sorry that I hurt you. I never, for one single second, thought of you as that type of girl. I wish you could look into my eyes and see what I do feel."

Summer stared into his eyes and her face softened. She took a deep breath and sighed. "Fine."

"Fine what?"

"I believe you care and—"

"You'll meet me later?" He gave her his best grin.

This time she graced him with a smile that curled his toes. "Yes."

He slowly let his breath out and smiled. "When later?" He could see the joy in her blue eyes.

"Later."

"Later, in the barn?"

"Holden, you forget you have four brothers. It will have to be much later. Besides aren't you tired from being out at all hours?"

"It wouldn't have taken so long if I hadn't been distracted by thoughts of your naked body."

She quickly glanced at Matt. "Shh."

Holden kissed her cheek. "Later," he whispered huskily. He walked back out of the house wearing a big grin. Later couldn't come fast enough for him. Maybe he'd work with Yukon for a while, that would keep him focused. A man could hope.

GIDDY WASN'T the right word but that was all Summer could come up with as to how she felt, and she wasn't quite sure why she wasn't still mad at Holden. She kept lecturing herself to stop thinking about Mindy Sue. She wasn't part of their equation. She had a right to be suspicious, especially after Brent, but Holden was an entirely different man. Oh and what a man he was. If he even rolled up his sleeves her stomach started to do flips. She never wanted anyone the way she wanted him. She wondered if he'd come to her room later. The anticipation had her unnerved. Her body began to feel the shiver of yearning, and her breasts felt heavy in need.

Damn, it was only midmorning. In the time she'd been there she'd gotten the place sparkling. It was a chore keeping it that way, but she was satisfied with her efforts. The sound of a truck horn caught her attention. Before she could even walk to the front window, Matt announced that Mindy Sue was here. Her heart panged. Damn didn't she just tell herself that she had nothing to fear from Mindy Sue?

Mindy Sue walked in and smiled at Matt. "I brought you more magazines. I could bring a book next time if you'd like."

Matt's eyes lit up and he smiled. "A few minutes of conversation would be great."

Mindy Sue's green hair was surprisingly flattering. It matched her outfit and her green and black striped nails. "Of course, sugar, I have all the time in the world for you. I've been meaning to stop by but trying to coordinate the names of owners with all their animals isn't easy. It would be easy if we had info. I'd have gotten it all into a database but we did a mass mailing and well it's still going to take time."

Summer relaxed. "Hi, Mindy Sue."

"Nice to see you again, Summer. I hear a lot about you every day."

Mindy Sue's words horrified Summer. The whole town was talking about her again. It chipped away at her self-esteem.

Mindy Sue must have noticed Summer's stricken look. "Oh no it's all good. I meant that Holden is always talking about you. In a nice way." She smiled at Summer. "I think he likes you."

Summer's face heated. It embarrassed her and thrilled her. "Can I get you something to drink? Are you hungry, it's almost lunch time?"

Mindy Sue looked to Matt for her answer.

"Yes, she's staying. She needs a bit of a rest from all that work she's been doing," Matt said.

"How about I set your plates where you are. It'll give you a small bit of privacy before the onslaught of O'Learys come in." Summer was rewarded with smiles from both.

A burden lifted off her shoulders. How she hadn't seen it before she didn't know. Matt and Mindy Sue liked each other. Happiness washed over her and hope filled the spot in her heart that had been reserved for jealousy.

As predicted Mark, Luke, John and Holden all came clambering in for lunch. It was one of the happiest meals she'd had there. The secret glances shared with Holden warmed her. Matt and Mindy Sue were happy in their own little world. The discussion revolved around horses but she hardly noticed. Holden's strong, handsome face was all she thought of.

His lips were delectable and she wanted them on her, anywhere, everywhere. Her body began to burn with desire and she felt restless.

"Holden, weren't you going to show me around the ranch?" She hoped he'd take the hint.

His eyebrows rose and he winked at her. "Did you want to go today? We could wait." The teasing glint in his eyes flustered her.

"Today, please," she said quickly then looked down at her plate. How could she be so brazen?

"Sounds good. I'll be back in a few."

Summer waited until the kitchen was empty before she looked up. Holden stood at the door staring at her. He tipped his hat, grinned and walked outside.

"You play video games?" She heard Mindy Sue ask Matt.

"Yes my favorite is Halo."

"Do you have the new one?"

Matt shook his head. "No, haven't had a chance to get that one yet."

Mindy Sue stood and touched his arm. "I'll bring it by next time." She bent and kissed Matt's cheek, waved goodbye to Summer and left.

Matt immediately glanced at Summer. "Think she likes me?"

"I wouldn't be surprised."

Matt's smile said it all. It was the happiest she'd ever seen him and her heart glowed. It reminded her of just how close she'd become to all of them.

Holden opened the door and made a beeline for her. He took her hand in his strong one and led her outside. "We have a tour I believe?"

Summer laughed. "Why, yes. I haven't seen much of your ranch."

Holden helped her into the truck and got in on his side. "It could take days to see it all properly." He gave her a wicked sidelong glance.

Summer lightly punched his shoulder. "We aren't really going to tour the ranch are we?"

His mouth opened in mock outrage. "I don't know what you mean."

"I hope you brought protection."

Holden laughed deeply. "Of course I did."

"Come to think of it you had some with you when you came to my room. Do you keep them in your wallet or something?"

Holden laughed even harder. "No, only when I'm around you."

His answer brightened her day. "So, where are we going first?"

"I figured you'd want to see my cattle."

"Cattle it is. Hurry, please."

"Anxious for some cowboy loving?"

Summer smiled. "You know I am!"

Holden turned off the road and headed toward a group of trees. "The hell with the cattle," he said, parking the truck. "I need to kiss you."

Before she could reply, he swooped down and claimed her lips. She immediately opened her mouth wanting the kiss to be as deep as possible. She sighed as Holden unclasped the front of her bra. Her breasts had wanted his lips on them all day.

He left her lips and kissed her neck. He nibbled her earlobe making her squirm. Sitting back for a second he pulled off her red t-shirt and white bra. The air on her breasts felt freeing. Holden continued his onslaught of kisses until he made his way to her breasts. He licked one and lightly squeezed the other. When he took the tip into his mouth to suck on it she moaned wildly with need.

"Feels so good, Holden." She reached and unbuttoned his shirt, his skin so smooth and soft under her fingertips. Running her hands through his dark chest hair, she kissed his shoulder, lightly nipping at him. She had no self-control when it came to Holden. She grabbed at his zipper and he leaned back against the seat invitingly.

Hurriedly she opened his pants, once again amazed how big and hard he was. She kissed, licked and kissed some more from his navel on down and was rewarded with an urgent gasp. After a minute he pulled her up from him and slipped her pants off. He wrapped his big warm hands around her waist and expertly planted her on top of him.

Her eyes widened as she took him all at once. It felt exhilarating. He made her feel so sexy. He held onto her waist guiding their rhythm and moved her up and down so fast, she grabbed his shoulders to keep her balance. Her hair splashed across her face as she rode. Holden was first to cry out, but he kept going until she spiraled to the sky and back. Wrapping his massive arms around her, he held her tight. The beat of his heart was pronounced against her. Summer wrapped her arms around him and treasured the feel of being held. She never wanted to move. Sitting on him was perfect.

"Like my tours?" he asked in a sultry voice.

Summer began to nod when she saw a truck out the rear

window. It was on the dirt road and she didn't recognize it. Her whole body automatically stiffened. "Holden." Her voice shook uncontrollably.

Holden lifted her off of him and turned around. "Stay down and get dressed as quickly as you can." He kept his gaze on the rear view window while he hustled to get himself dressed. He didn't bother with his shirt. He leaned down and reached under the seat, bringing out a rifle.

Summer gasped at the sight of it. "He's just staring at us."

"Get your head down." Holden reached to open his door. "He's gone, hold on. Put your seatbelt on. I'm going after him."

Summer didn't reply she just did what he said. They heard a thump as Holden tried to back up. He immediately got out of the truck and swore. Summer watched as he got on his cell phone.

The fury on his face when he came back inside the truck scared her. "We won't be going anywhere for a while."

"Wh-What do you mean?"

"That bastard got close enough to us to put an icepick into the back tire. Damn it!" Holden hit the steering wheel. "I could have gotten you killed."

"No, Holden, don't blame yourself. We'll just have to be careful and more aware."

There didn't seem to be anything she could do to break the tension in the truck. At least she knew that it wasn't directed toward her. "Did you call the sheriff?"

"No, I called Mark and Jonas. I'm going to need help keeping you safe."

Summer nodded her stomach in knots while they waited for backup.

THE CAVALRY ARRIVED. Jonas reached them first, then Mark. Jonas took Summer home, while Mark helped Holden change the tire.

Jonas drove her home in silence. She made no attempt at conversation. The thoughts whirling in her head made it impossible to focus

The boys were all on the front porch and the worried expressions on the boys' face hurt her heart. She never intended to bring them any harm and someone was bound to get hurt with Brent out there. The fact that he was so close to them hadn't sunk in yet.

Colt and Caleb showed up, at the house, both kissing her on the cheek. Stone pulled up next. scowling as he walked toward them. Finally, Holden and Mark returned.

Holden led her to a leather chair in the great room next to Matt and promptly forgot about her as the men proposed different plans of attack. She tried to say something once but they didn't really acknowledge her. Frustrated, she finally yelled, "Stop it!"

They all looked at her with puzzled expressions except for Holden. He just frowned.

"Summer, let us take care of this." Holden's curtness grated.

"Holden, I'm not some lap dog you can set on a chair and forget. This is about me."

Caleb walked over and sat on the arm of her chair. He always had a calming way about him. "I know it seems like we're taking over. Frankly, we are, but not only for your protection. Holden and his brothers need help too." He nudged her shoulder with his lean hip. "Besides we like to impress the ladies." His grin was infectious and the next thing she knew she grinned back.

"It's time for a new sheriff." Stone suggested.

"Too bad it's not election time," Jonas commented, shaking his head.

Holden studied each man. "I know you all have your own places to work and I don't want to put this on your shoulders. If you'd just give me and my brothers some ideas, we can take it from there."

Jonas' laugh boomed from his broad chest. "You are new around here, Holden. We take care of our own, that includes neighbors. Besides you're the only vet around. We can't have anything happen to you."

Holden's Adam's apple bobbed as he swallowed. "I appreciate it."

Colt's dark eyes looked into Summer's. "If he wanted you harmed he had the chance today."

She automatically nodded. Everything was finally sinking in and she shivered. The thought of Brent being so close to them made her ill. Did he watch? What did he want? He was bound to get caught if he stayed around town.

Lost in thought, Summer was surprised to see everyone standing and shaking hands. They all said goodbye to her and she smiled with a quick nod. Her mind became jumbled. The chance to relish in Holden's love-making had passed. Why was Brent after her? She must have missed something. How could she have been with a murderer and not pick up any clues? He must have shown some sign of his true self. Glancing up, she became aware of Holden's intense stare. She took comfort in the concern in his eyes. He cared about her and it warmed her heart. She hoped that her return gaze held the warmth she felt for him, but she wasn't sure.

"Are you alright, honey?" His five o'clock shadow on his strong jaw made him look roguishly handsome. His voice sounded deep and sexy.

She nodded unsure of herself. Unsure of everything.

"What about the State Police?" She clasped her hands together to still the trembling.

"Jonas said that they won't get involved without the sheriff's backing. Is there something you're not telling me?" He suddenly found the floor more interesting to look at. Summer wavered between wanting to rail at him and wanting his comfort. What did he mean? Her mouth formed an O. "You think I took part in all this don't you?" She slapped her shaking hand over her mouth, horrified.

Without glancing at her, Holden turned and walked to the window, keeping his back to her. He was hiding. Her stomach turned, and her throat began to burn with unshed tears. Enough was enough, she was tired of being accused of such horrendous crimes. How could he make love to her and then think her in cahoots with Brent? "I'll stay with Caleb and Colt."

"No." He didn't turn around.

She looked around the room at the boys. They were all uncharacteristically silent. Matt and Mark refused to meet her gaze. Luke's eyes gave away his grief and John looked as though someone had kicked him. "Then I'll stay with Jonas. He probably needs some help."

"Jonas doesn't want you." Holden still looked out the window. His hollow tone of voice made her wince.

"So, no one wants me. It doesn't matter." The tears on her face showed her lie.

Finally, Holden turned his face full of rage. "It does matter. That bastard Brent would not be around these parts if he had what he wanted. He'd have to be crazy to take such a risk unless you have the money or some evidence against him."

His dark eyes flashed as he spoke and it tore her heart. The nightmare that started that night at the bar refused to end. "I was brought up in a decent family. We had morals and respect and love. I am not a liar, I am not a thief and I am most certainly not going to stick around here to be kicked around."

John rushed toward her and gave her a hug around her waist. He held on to her, anchoring her. "I don't want you to leave."

His pleading eyes were too much. Summer hugged him back. She had just promised to stay and here she was planning to leave. Did keeping her word trump keeping her dignity?

"I don't want you to leave either," Luke spoke up. He walked toward her and stood at her side glaring at Holden.

Holden shook his head. "Guys I need to talk to Summer, alone." His gaze upon her was piercing. "Summer, will you go upstairs with me so we can talk in private?"

She nodded slowly. What the hell? Things needed to be settled one way or the other and it would be better if the boys didn't hear what she was sure Holden had to say. She gently drew away from John and gave Luke a slight smile. "It's fine guys. Holden and I do need to talk."

Their worried expressions ate at her. They were all too young to be mixed up in her problems. Sometimes the best thing you could do for a person was leave and maybe this was one of those times. She turned and walked up the stairs to her bedroom.

Summer peered out her window and leaned her brow against the warm glass, waiting for Holden. She didn't want to see the doubt in his dark eyes, eyes that recently were filled with desire and, she had hoped, much more. What a difference a few hours could make. The longer she waited, the angrier she became. She wasn't responsible and she hadn't done anything wrong. If Holden had seen her battered body after the attack, he wouldn't doubt her. Her word alone was not enough; she obviously required proof. It galled her to no end and she was damned no matter what she decided to do. Taking a deep breath she realized it wasn't her decision. She turned as she heard Holden enter the room. He slowly closed the door and leaned back against it, leaving a wide chasm between them.

He took her measure and from his expression she knew she came up short. She tried to tell herself it didn't matter but her heart shattered anyway. One by one the pain of each piece impaled her until she hurt so badly, she couldn't stand. Summer sat at the end of her bed, facing him. She refused to be a coward. She hadn't done anything wrong. Why didn't he just ask her to leave? His silence was killing her. "You don't have to say it, Holden. It's written all over your face."

"You have no idea what I'm thinking, Summer. I don't want you to leave."

Summer frowned. "I'm not buying it, Holden. I'm in a tough spot. Those boys downstairs don't want me to leave, but how can I stay knowing you suspect me?" She bit her bottom lip so hard she tasted blood. Her hands were clenching the quilt she sat on.

"I shouldn't have questioned you in front of my brothers. That wasn't right. I'm sorry."

"That's it? We have sex. Brent gets close enough to kill us. You think I have the money that was taken, which pretty much implies I murdered Paul and all you can say is you shouldn't have asked me in front of the boys?" Summer stood and quickly closed the gap between them. "I am innocent. I would think that you of all people would give me the benefit of the doubt. I'm not leaving. I promised those boys I wouldn't. I just ask that you stay out of my way."

He crossed his arms in front of her and cocked his right eyebrow. "Is that the way you want it? Fine, I'll give you a wide berth." He turned and opened the door. Without looking back he quietly closed it behind him.

Damn! It hadn't really solved anything. If anything it made things worse. Her body trembled in longing, and her heart cried for what could have been, what should have been. Regret washed over her and she wished she could just climb into bed and pull the quilt up over her head, but that wasn't her. She reminded herself that she was a strong, capable, innocent woman. She stood taller and dashed all tears from her face with the heels of her hands. She had nothing to hide, nothing to be ashamed of and she'd be damned if she'd allow anyone to treat her as if she had.

She didn't intend to play the victim but hell, a little bit of kindness her way would be nice. No, no running. She was going to go straight down those stairs and do what she was hired to do. She was going to feed those boys.

Standing tall with her shoulders back she walked down the stairs. All eyes were on her, except for Holden's. He was glaringly absent. Without saying a word she started making dinner.

HOLDEN KICKED the wooden side of the barn. He strode into the tack room, after stomping out of the house, telling his brothers to stay inside. Damn it all to hell! His big mouth got him in trouble again. Where was his filter when he needed it? He accused Summer of being part of murder. He'd kick the wall again if it hadn't been hurt so much the first time. The look in her eyes, he'd never forget it. He hurt and betrayed her.What the hell was wrong with him? He paced back and forth in the small room until he heard Yukon, sounding agitated. He knew shouldn't have come into the barn. He should have realized that the animals would be affected. What kind of vet was he anyway? If he could kick himself instead of the barn he would.

He half listened for Summer's car. He couldn't expect her to stay. He wanted—needed—to apologize but their emotions were too heightened and he didn't think she'd listen. He leaned his elbows on the sturdy wooden table and buried his face in his hands. What a day. It had gone from the best to the worst. Having Summer in his arms had been pure pleasure. The joy on her pretty face and the spark in her blue eyes while they made love amazed and humbled him. His heart had been filled with her essence and now it languished, empty. Maybe he did think she had something to do with it. It made sense. Why would that jerk Brent stick around if he wasn't expecting something from Summer? Holden stood and pounded his fist against the table. Holding his throbbing hand, he headed out of the barn. He had brothers to raise and a practice to attend to and Summer to protect. Maybe she'd be calmer when he went into the house.

That hope was quickly dashed as soon as his boots hit the wooden floor. She turned from the kitchen lifted her chin and gave him a sour look. He scowled back at her. This was not going to be easy. Her eyes hardened at his scowl and he swore under his breath. He didn't mean to scowl at her. Jackass of the year came to mind. Taking a deep breath he tried to smile. "So what's up guys?"

Matt just gave him a blank look, Mark ignored him altogether. Luke and John were in the kitchen. They both turned and smiled.

"Summer is teaching us how to make spaghetti," Luke told him.

John nodded. "It's what every bachelor should know and guess what?"

"What?" Holden asked.

"It doesn't come out of a can. I always thought it came out of a can. Didn't you think that too, John?" Luke looked at his younger brother.

116

John glanced up away from the pots on the stove. "Yeah, we've only had the can stuff. This smells much better."

The side of Holden's mouth quirked up. "Yes it does. Now what's this bachelor stuff?" He hoped that his lightened voice would break the tension.

Luke and John exchanged glances and smiled. Luke spoke. "Well the way to a man's heart is his stomach. That's what we thought."

"We were so wrong," John added, shaking his head.

Holden's eyebrows rose. "Oh?"

Summer looked up at him, he could see the humor in her eyes. She made his heart jump.

John walked over to him. "You see, women like a man who knows how to cook and stuff. Did you know that there is no such thing as woman's work? I could have sworn you told us that cooking was really women's work."

His face heated a bit. "I guess I did say that but I was wrong and it appears that I've been wrong about a lot of things lately." He was rewarded with a brief nod from Summer.

John ran back next to Summer. "I didn't miss anything did I?"

Luke touched her arm and got her attention. "You're not leaving are you?"

Summer graced Luke with a smile. "No, I'll be here." Her voice was quiet but they all heard it.

Relief washed over him and he silently thanked God. His phone rang. He was needed out at Stone's place, so he grabbed his bag and his Stetson, turning to say goodbye to Summer She had turned her back to him. He hesitated.

"I'll save you some." She still hadn't turned, but at least she acknowledged him.

THERE WAS LITTLE LEFT to save. Jonas came by to visit. His wanting to get to know his neighbors act didn't fool her. Summer knew that Holden had sent him over, but she played along anyway. Jonas was a shy man and she was sure he didn't relish spending his evening drinking coffee with her in the kitchen.

Every time she saw him, his size surprised her. His shoulders were broad enough to fill a doorway and he was very tall. His amber eyes were kind, but she could sense pain in them. His brown hair was very short, almost military style. He wasn't one for making conversation and to her dismay, she kept blathering on about stuff. After a while she didn't even know what they were talking about. Finally, she just stopped talking and they sat in a companionable silence, listening to the boys play video games and vying for turns.

"You know they do make one with four controllers."

Summer almost jumped. "Oh I didn't know. That would solve a lot of problems."

"Yep." Jonas nodded.

Silence again. "You don't have to stay and babysit, Jonas."

He appeared surprised. "I don't know what you mean."

Tempted to laugh she looked at the floor, pretending to find it fascinating until the urge passed. "Are you planning on visiting until Holden gets back?"

Finally, he smiled. "Yep."

"Okay then. Usually I go and take a shower before bed. The bathroom is so crowded in the mornings. This house is wonderful and updated except for the bathrooms. Is it rude if I go and take a shower and try to get some sleep?"

Jonas smiled again. "You go right ahead, Summer. Relax anyway you can. You can rest assured that I will be here."

"That's what I figured. It is nice to visit with you, Jonas. We must do this more often." Summer stood, put her mug in the sink and touched Jonas' shoulder. "Thank you."

Jonas swallowed hard apparently uncomfortable with her touch. "Goodnight."

Summer took her shower and as she headed toward her room she could hear Jonas' voice along with the others wanting turns at the game. He had a good heart. She wished that she could get to know him better. She prayed that one day he'd find someone to take his pain away.

Sliding into bed, she hoped for sleep but she tossed and turned reliving the day's events. Mostly, she relived the passion they had found in Holden's truck. He was an amazing lover and he'd brought her to heights she never dreamed of. Her body throbbed remembering how he filled her. She pictured herself astride him, his mouth on her breast while she threaded her fingers through his hair. Her head, heart and body all warred against each other. When the sun started to rise, she still hadn't slept. Summer slipped out of bed and looked in the mirror. Her blue eyes were bloodshot and her honey blonde hair had seen better days. It looked as though she had wrestled with a tiger all night. She quickly brushed it and pulled it back into a ponytail. Throwing on a pair of jean shorts and a purple t-shirt, she padded barefoot down the stairs, coming to a halt at the smell the fresh coffee. She wasn't sure she was up to seeing Holden so early in the morning. Determined to make things work for his brothers' sakes, she plodded ahead.

He'd been leaning over the kitchen sink, staring out the window. He turned when she entered the kitchen. It didn't appear that he'd gotten any sleep either. His eyes had circles under them and his black hair stuck up all over. If it had been any other day she would have teased him about it.

"Looks like it's going to be a nice day," she commented as she poured herself a cup of coffee.

"It sure does." He gave her a sad smile. "Listen, Summer—"

She held her hand up, her palm facing him. "No, I don't want to hear it. Let's just try to make the best of it for the boy's' sake. That's what really matters."

His stare was so intent she felt as though he was looking into her soul.

"You care about them."

"I love them, Holden. Each one of them. I'm concerned for their safety but I'm also concerned how they would feel if I left again. I don't want to be the reason they distrust women."

Holden nodded. "I understand and you're right. They need constancy in their lives. They've just been uprooted from Texas."

The hitch in his throat when he said Texas caught her attention. They never did say why they had to move. A mystery best saved for later. She had enough on her plate.

"So, besides having Jonas come and protect me, what is the game plan?"

"I'm hiring extra hands to help with the cattle and other chores. I want my brothers closer to the house. I'll have them work with the horses. I'd lock you in your room but I have a feeling you wouldn't stay, so I hired a couple men to act as bodyguards."

Her eyes widened. "All of that? Holden you can't put out that kind of cash. In ranching you have to save for the bad years."

"Don't worry about it."

"I do worry. What are you being paid as a vet? I heard Mrs. Grandy paid you in chickens a few days ago."

Holden graced her with a smile. "She did. Seeing as I have no use for chickens I give them to Mrs. Ruth. Then when Mrs. Ruth needs my services she pays me the same chickens and I give them back to Mrs. Grandy."

Summer couldn't help the bubble of laughter that erupted. "You're kidding me."

"I wish I were. They are both cute little ladies. I think they are just lonely. Mrs. Grandy's horse, Jasper, is old but fine. She calls me out there at least once a week and Mrs. Ruth's dog Penny is fine too."

She gazed at the handsome planes of his face. He really was a good man. "I don't want to bankrupt you. It's my problem."

"Just humor me, Summer. Can you do that? Please?"

She took a sip of her cooling coffee, watching him. Finally, she nodded. "Yes, I can do that."

The warm smile she received was worth agreeing with him. She almost smiled back, but she remembered that he didn't fully believe her. Holden set his mug down. "I need to go to the clinic for a few hours. I'll call before sending anyone new out here. Can I get you to agree to stay close to the house today?"

"Sure." She watched him walk away. He stopped at the couch and chatted with Matt. Holden was doing most of the talking. Matt was nodding. Probably instructions to keep the boys close by.

Breakfast needed to be made.

LATER THAT DAY, Summer surveyed the motley crew of hands Holden had sent out. He did call before each arrival. There were five of them each looked tough and well-seasoned. She wondered where he found these men. She hadn't seen them before. Maybe he broke them out of jail. They didn't look like cow hands and they only went by first names.

The oldest one was Jaz. He looked to be fifty years old. He

was a bit on the short side and bald. His blue eyes had a "don't mess with me" look in them. Next Gabe arrived. He was taller than most and wider than anyone she'd known, even Jonas, and just as beefy. He'd probably be good at arm wrestling. He had the whole tall, dark, almost handsome thing going for him, but there were no smiles in that man's heart.

Ben was very polite but he refused to make eye contact. He seemed shifty to her. He too was tall and truck like.

Denver appeared non-threatening until she saw all the tattoos around his neck. There was something not right about that man.

Sly had the look of the devil about him. He had small dark eyes, dark hair and was a bit on the thin side. He made eye contact with her and she got the chills. Yes, definitely the devil. She wondered if they even rode horses. She didn't know what to do with them except feed them. She made them sandwiches and coffee. They might have made her uncomfortable but they weren't disrespectful. The sound of a truck coming up the drive made her anxious and she hoped it was Holden.

She went to the front window and there were several trucks coming her way. The men all got up from the table, and headed outside. Ben stopped to thank her for lunch before he reached the door.

"Matt, do you know what the heck is going on?"

"Holden bought six new ATVs to make it easier to get around the ranch."

"Are those men really ranch hands?"

Matt shrugged his shoulders. "I guess so. They do look like a hardened lot."

"Here, let me help you outside so we can see what's going on." Summer helped Matt up and handed him his crutches. She held the door open as he hobbled his way to the porch. They both sat in the wooden chairs. Summer didn't want to call attention to herself but she did want to know what the plan was.

Holden directed the men and answered questions, outlining their jobs. Being a leader came naturally to him. His confidence was downright sexy and Summer found herself feeling bereft, certain that they would never find their way back to each other. At least not the way they were. "Are you all right?" Matt asked.

Summer pulled her gaze away from Holden. "Yes, why do you ask?"

"There's sadness about you when you look at my brother. I thought, well I guess I don't know what I thought." His perusal of her was intense and it made her face heat.

"I don't know what is going on. I thought what you thought, but things didn't work out but it's fine, really.

Matt gave her a searching look before he turned his head and watched the ATVs being unloaded. She closed her eyes and took a deep breath. She needed to learn to hide her feelings better. From now on she was going to portray the happy, easy going housekeeper. She'd do her job and watch out for the boys. There was no way she could keep from loving them and she didn't plan to pull back from them. She found she needed them as much as they needed her. It felt nice to have an anchor.

CHAPTER NINE

A few days later, all she wanted was to be able to walk out of the house alone. The tension in her body begged for release and she didn't know what to do. Men were in and out of the house at all hours wanting to be fed. They were all nice enough but good Lord; whenever she went toward the door she got the look of the devil from them.

Holden hadn't been around the last few days. While compiling their database of horse owners, he'd come across a few that were not supposed to have horses due to past abuse. He did take time for his brothers though. They were lucky to have him. It made her warm inside, yet it made her so lonely she wanted to cry. He nodded to her a couple times but that was all.

A wide berth, that's what she was getting from him. It's what she wanted, wasn't it? He'd often come home in the wee hours of the morning. She heard him in the room across the hall and she had to fight the temptation to go and jump in bed with him. It wouldn't solve anything.

All this waiting for Brent was crazy. There hadn't been a

KATHLEEN BALL

sighting of him since they'd seen him from the truck. She'd
gone over every date, every conversation she'd had with
Brent trying to find some clue. Did he leave her something
he wanted back? He really didn't talk about his past. He
regaled her with stories of what was happening at the
Winders' ranch where he had worked.

She knew that Jonas had talked with Dave Winders at
length but nothing turned up. Everyone had thought Brent
to be a standup guy. In one way that made her feel better.
Maybe she wasn't such a bad judge of character after all.
Summer shook her head, the jury was still out on that. Look
at the mess she'd made with Holden.

She glanced at Ben and Denver, eating breakfast in the
kitchen. They were nice enough but she was beginning to
feel like a short order cook. She needed to get groceries. The
thought of that didn't make her happy. The people in town
probably thought the worst with all this mess.

"Good morning, Summer." Holden's deep voice startled
her and she quickly turned.

"I'll have your breakfast for you in a minute." She walked
toward to kitchen but she didn't get far. Holden snaked his
arms around her waist from behind and drew her back
against him.

"We need to go into town today," he said and she turned
her head to see him. "It was Jonas' idea but it's a good one.
We are going to spend the day in town and see if anything
shakes loose."

What was he doing? Her stomach clenched at the thought
of a whole day in town. "I, we need groceries but other than
that— I thought you didn't particularly like me."

Holden kissed the side of her neck. His breath was so
warm. "Trust me."

She couldn't think as he nipped at her earlobe. "Are you
sure?"

He turned her in his arms and gazed down at her. His dark eyes seemed sincere. "Someone must know something. One theory is that someone hired Brent to kill Paul."

Her eyes widened. "But he was the sweetest man."

He gave her a reassuring smile. "I'm sure he was. Let's go to town and see what happens. If we act the happy couple, we're bound to be noticed by Beverly at least."

Summer stiffened and gave him a curt nod. "Let me go brush my hair and I'll be ready." She turned to go, and turned back. "You haven't had breakfast."

"I know, just hurry."

The stairs appeared insurmountable but she took one step at a time. The squeezing of her heart turned into agony. Pretend. How was she supposed to pretend to be a happy couple when her whole heart wanted it to be the truth? In the bathroom, she grabbed her hairbrush and quickly ran it through her hair. Taking a deep breath, she studied herself in the mirror and the pain in her eyes obvious. It wouldn't do to let anyone know how she really felt. She closed her eyes and slowly let out her breath, trying to calm herself. When they opened, it was a relief that some of the distress had disappeared.

THEY RODE IN COMPANIONABLE SILENCE. Holden glanced at Summer many times trying to decipher her feelings but she didn't glance back. She was bound to be nervous.

"You know I haven't seen much of the town except for my clinic." There was no answer. "I've seen the community center where that librarian, Beverly, seems to be at all hours. Carlston is a nice little town. It was luck a veterinarian was needed here. Have you eaten at Lucy's Deli?"

"I grew up here, Holden."

"Right." Talking seemed to be out of the question. Holden parked the truck in front of Lucy's Deli and got out. He rounded the truck to grab Summer's door but she was already out and on the sidewalk. She gave him a questioning glare.

He shrugged his shoulders. "I'm hungry. I didn't eat breakfast."

Summer rolled her eyes and walked ahead of him. She hesitated at the door. Holden reached around her and opened it, ushering her in. He hoped for a welcoming reception. He wanted to get something to eat, and he needed people to see Summer. He tipped his hat and nodded when Lucy came from behind the counter and smiled at them. She had blonde hair pulled back into a braid. She appeared to be about thirty and she had kind hazel eyes.

"Well, it's good to see you, Summer." Lucy hugged Summer, and Holden wanted to laugh at the total surprise on Summer's face.

"Thank you," Summer murmured as she took a step back out of the embrace.

"You two take a seat and I'll bring some coffee over."

Holden smiled and led Summer to a booth at the front window. He smiled when she scowled at him. "We want to see the town."

"I guess you're right." She slid into the booth and grabbed the menu.

"Hold your head up, Summer. You did nothing wrong."

She stared at him, studying him as if she were searching for the truth of his statement. She sat back against the booth straight and tall. She tilted her chin up a bit. "That's the first good idea I've heard all day."

He threw his head back and laughed. God, she was amazingly beautiful. He wanted nothing more than to get all of the ugliness done with so they could start their lives. He almost added together to his last thought but decided he didn't know if she'd even have him anymore.

"What's wrong? First you laugh and now you look as though you've lost your best friend."

"Nothing really, I just want this to be over."

"Me too."

Lucy was kind and served them a great breakfast. Holden kept alert at all times, scanning each customer. He saw some dirty looks thrown their way but there were also smiles of encouragement. No one bothered them until Lizzie Hoff entered. Holden wanted to groan aloud. Lizzie thought she was the local society matron. He was pretty sure the society consisted of two members, Lizzie and Beverly. He willed her to move by them but they were not so lucky.

"Hello, Holden. I thought you got rid of her." Lizzie nodded her black haired head toward Summer.

"Why would you think that?" He smiled at the old bitty.

"I believe that Beverly gave you enough reasons. You can't have her kind around your brothers. What if the Department of Social Services were to find out? She's living there with you isn't she?" She folded her arms in front of her and tapped her foot.

Holden saw that Summer was about to say something so he kicked her lightly in the shin. If he read her expression right, he could expect payback.

"Lizzie, you don't need to worry your pretty little head about my family. I appreciate your concern but you see, you have it all wrong. Summer here is a wonderful, honest woman."

"Humph. Well, all I can say is I tried. I'll be the first to say I told you so."

Holden smiled. "I'm sure you will. If you'll excuse us we were having a nice conversation."

Lizzie glared at Summer, then at Holden. Finally, she sat at a table far away from them.

He reached across the table, took Summer's small, dainty hand in his and was relieved she didn't pull away, "She's just a meddlesome, old bitty."

Summer suddenly began to laugh. "Thank you for defending me."

"Anytime. Let's get out of here. We have a whole town to explore."

Summer downed the rest of her coffee and stood. "Fine, if we have to."

Thanking Lucy on their way out, Holden quickly took Summer's hand in his and led her down the street. They passed Rex's Barber Shop. It still had the old barber's pole outside of it. Next they walked by the community center. Beverly walked out the door and stared at them the whole time while Holden smiled. Then they walked to the general store and he stopped. "Let's go in."

Summer shrugged and followed him inside. It was a huge store owned by Paul's brother Andy Gallagher. You could find everything ranging from hunting supplies to cocktail dresses. The bell over the door rang as they entered. Andy glanced up from the papers he was reading at the checkout counter. His red hair was graying, his blue eyes looked dull and when he came out from behind the counter you could tell he was a man who enjoyed his food.

"Oh, Summer, it is so good to see you. You look much better than the last time…"

"Thanks, Andy. You know Holden O'Leary don't you?"

Andy reached out and shook Holden's hand. "Anyone with animals knows this young man. I have to warn you, I don't take chickens as payment." He chuckled.

He turned toward Summer. "Is Holden here taking good care of you? I've been worried about you. Paul would have wanted to be sure you were faring well. He thought of you as a daughter."

A tear threatened to roll down her face. "I'm fine. Holden and his brothers have made me feel like part of their family."

"Good. I'll let you shop."

There was something about Andy that seemed off to Holden. He didn't seem to be genuine in his concern for Summer. He wanted to question her about it but decided to wait until they got home. Instead he walked right over to the dresses and started looking. Summer followed him, frowning. "What are you doing?"

"I've been invited to the Carlston Summer Social. I wanted to ask a certain young woman to the dance but I don't think she has a dress. Maybe you could help me pick one out for her."

Summer glared at him. Next thing he knew she kicked him in his shin, hard.

"Hey what was that for?"

"You expect me to pick out a dress for your date?"

"I'm no good at this, I thought you got the hint. It's you I want to take to the dance." He lifted her chin with his finger and peered into her eyes. "Summer Fitzgerald, would you do me the honor of being my date for the Summer Social?"

Her glare softened until she smiled at him. "I'd be delighted. I can buy my own dress."

"I know you can, but oh hell I don't want to hash it out here. Let's get what you need and worry about it later."

Summer nodded. "No need to spoil the day." She picked a green dress from the rack. "Do you like this one?"

"No."

Summer frowned. "Why not?"

"It'll look too good on you." He kept a straight face and grabbed a sack like blue dress and held it in front of him. "This matches your eyes."

She appeared dumbfounded. Then her eyes narrowed. "I'll take the green one." She walked away toward the shoes.

She was going to look damn sexy in that green dress. He was going to have to keep the other men away. He looked at the blue dress again. Sighing, he put it back on the rack and followed her to the shoe department. Her brow furrowed as she examined the sparse selection. "I don't know. I usually wear my boots or sneakers." She picked up a pair of high heeled shoes. "What about these?"

"Try them on."

Summer sat on one of the chairs near the shoes and took off her boots. She slipped the shoes on and stood. She took a step and wobbled. Frowning, she took another step. "You'd think at my age I'd have worn high heels before. I'd ask you what you think but you don't seem to have any taste in women's clothes."

His laugh started as a slow rumble and grew. "Sweetheart, is it a crime that I don't want anyone else to even look at you? That there dress is too eye catching."

Frowning more, she studied him. "What's that supposed to mean? It covers everything it's supposed to. Do you think it's not appropriate?"

He'd stepped in it again. "I mean that you will look lovely and I don't want anyone else to dance with you."

Summer blushed as the corners of her mouth turned up. "Really? I've been under the impression we were done."

"What else do you need? I like the heels." He desperately changed the subject. Of course they weren't done. Hell, he'd hardly gotten warmed up but the general store was not the place to talk about it.

"Why won't you talk to me? Were those kisses this morning a ploy to get me to come to town with you?" Her eyes grew misty as she took the heels off, put her boots back on and grabbed the shoebox. She haphazardly put the shoes in the box and made her way to the counter.

Andy grinned at Summer. Holden had been aware that Andy stood close enough to hear them the whole time. He wondered what was up. Maybe he was concerned for Summer but somehow his gut told him that wasn't the reason.

Holden paid while Summer insisted that she would pay him back as soon as they got home. He had no intention of taking her money but he smiled and nodded at her to keep her from fussing. She hadn't seemed so stubborn when he first met her.

Finally, they stopped at Ander's Food Mart. Mr. Ander followed them around the whole store. Holden kept glaring at him but he wouldn't go away. They grabbed some food and left. At least he didn't say anything to Summer and he didn't call the sheriff. Maybe it was a successful shopping trip after all.

He loaded the bags into the truck. "Ready to go home?"

"Yes, I'm done here for a while. I sure wanted to hit Anders with the cart. He's a jerk. Well, he's the sheriff's best friend so I guess he believes I'm involved. I'm having second thoughts about the social. If people don't want me around, I don't want to make others uncomfortable. There could be trouble."

Holden opened the door for her and smiled. "Don't worry so much." He got in the truck and glanced at her. She had her head rested on the back of the seat with her eyes closed. He'd never noticed how long her eyelashes were. Reaching out he caressed her cheek with the back of his hand and she rewarded him with a smile.

"Trouble I can handle, Summer. You thinking I don't want you concerns me more."

She opened her eyes then her mouth. Holden put his finger on her lips.

"Just listen for a minute. I care about you. Care isn't the word I'm looking for. I know I've been distant and I'm sorry. I doubted you and I'm sorrier than I can say. Oh hell, what I'm trying to say is that I'm falling in love with you and I don't know what to do about it."

She swallowed hard. "Really? I've felt so alone for so long and your doubts shattered me. I thought I saw something in your eyes that said you cared about me and I hoped I was right. I'm half in love with you too. I've been wrestling with myself because I didn't know if it was a good thing or not. I don't want to get hurt. My heart can't take any more disappointment. You didn't see me all battered. I don't remember much but I still have this fear in me and you keep the fear away. I've never known a man like you. You've given so much of yourself to your brothers and to animals."

His heart beat faster, her words were pure magic and he felt himself falling more in love with her. She never acted as though she was afraid but he was glad that he made her feel safe. "Let's go home. Maybe we can find some privacy sometime."

Summer laughed. "Good luck with that. You hired men to watch me remember?"

Nodding, he started the truck and began to drive. He reached over and took her hand in his. For a moment he forgot about Brent and the threats they all faced.

Upon arriving home, Summer waited for Holden to open her door, wanting to feel his hands on her when he helped her down. The bright sun showed the golden highlights in his dark hair. It illuminated one side of his face emphasizing his high cheekbones and strong jaw. She made sure that their bodies brushed against each other. Intense desire flared in his eyes and warmed her heart.

They weren't alone for long. Everyone came out to help bring in packages. Matt supervised from the front porch. She gave Holden a smile before they were separated due to all the help they were getting. Before she knew it, she was in the kitchen putting groceries away while Holden huddled with Jaz and Gabe. Strategizing no doubt. She'd be happy when it was all over. She wanted Brent out of her life.

The phone rang and she answered it. Someone named Sheila was calling for Holden and her Texas Twang was very pronounced. The surprised expression on his face was immediately followed by anger.

"Tell her not to call here again."

Summer stared at him. Why couldn't he tell Miss Texas? She did what he asked and hung up the phone.

"What did she say?" Holden asked.

"A lot of words that I refuse to repeat. Next time tell her yourself." The house was silent. All eyes were on Holden. His brothers looked worried. Maybe Sheila was the key to his past. Holden just nodded and went back to talking with Jaz and Gabe. This time his cell phone rang. She watched him answer it. She couldn't hear what he said but he nodded a few times.

"I gotta go. Jacob Ash just bought five horses at auction. I need to get over there before he tries to ship them out of the country. Damn, he's on a watch list."

Summer tried to gauge whether or not he was telling the truth. Maybe Sheila had his cellphone number. She couldn't let her mind go there. He was going to rescue horses and that was that.

She was so deep in thought she hardly noticed him walking to her until he was in arms reach. He put his hands on her waist and reeled her in. He swooped down, kissed her and left. Summer touching her lips. They still tingled after he went out the front door. Everyone was giving her a little smile and she felt her face grow warm. "What?"

Everyone went about their business until she was left with Matt and Ben. Ben, she assumed, was the bodyguard of the day. When was this all going to end?

Collecting the laundry she thought about her conversation with Holden. Her heart skipped a beat remembering his words. Love was a good thing. She hoped love was a good thing. Imagine a man like Holden falling for her. She walked by a mirror and studied her face. Maybe she was pretty enough. She stood straighter realizing that Holden was the lucky one. She smiled at her reflection. Her self-esteem was coming back.

A WEEK LATER, Holden paced in front of the stairs, waiting for Summer to come down. It was the night of the Summer Social and he couldn't wait to see her in that green dress. It'd been a long week with no privacy. He'd hardly gotten a kiss in and he needed much more than a kiss. No matter what, he planned to sneak into her room tonight.

He'd mentioned it but Summer was concerned that his brothers would find out. Holden had wanted to roll his eyes at her but he pretended to understand. He tried to touch her at every opportunity. She'd smile then pretend he wasn't there. He would never understand women.

Summer came down the stairs and one look at her in the green dress and he forgot all about trying to understand her. "Wow, you look great!"

She blushed and smiled with pleasure. "Look, I can walk in my heels. I've been practicing."

He couldn't stop staring at her. The green dress hugged her body. It had tiny straps to hold it up and he hoped they stayed put. It was cut a bit lower than what she usually wore. He liked it yet it worried him. Her blond hair was piled on top of her head with little wisps of hair curling down. Her neck looked sexy. Hell, everything about her screamed sexy.

"We could still go and buy that blue one," he suggested, only half kidding.

"You look very handsome yourself." From the sparkle in her blue eyes he could tell she meant it.

"We all do," John said. "Let's go, I don't want to miss any of the food."

Summer laughed and grabbed her wrap, which Holden helped put on. His hands settled on her shoulders and she turned and gazed up at him. There were promises in her expression that he planned to have her keep.

They piled into two trucks and off they went. Holden couldn't wait to dance with Summer. She was all he thought about and it was making him crazy. Last week when he'd gone to rescue the horses from Jacob Ash, they had found signs of someone living in his barn. They watched the place but Brent never showed. He didn't tell Summer.

"We're being followed," Summer told him. He reached out and took her hand. "It's Denver and Gabe." Some of her happiness seemed to fade. "When will this be over?"

"I don't know, honey. I wish I knew."

He parked the car in the community center's parking lot. It was supposedly from one of the original buildings in Carlston. He helped her out of the truck by lifting her at the waist and setting her down in front of him. She wobbled for a second in her new shoes. "Ready?"

Smiling, she took the arm he offered and they walked in. The room was filled with round tables, covered with green and yellow table cloths. There was a stage in the back of the room with a band playing. To the right, tables were laden down with food. His brothers immediately headed right to them.

He held Summer's hand and started to lead her to an empty table. Unfortunately Beverly Rain waylaid them. He wanted gag from her perfume. She must have used extra tonight.

"I thought you got rid of her. She really isn't welcome here you know." Beverly had the type of voice that carried and soon everyone was staring at them.

Lizzie Hoff immediately came to Beverly's side. Lizzie wore a strapless black dress that made her skin look pasty white. "I'm surprised you came, my dear." She looked Summer up and down, and then scowled.

Summer's hand trembled in his and he gave it a quick squeeze. "No one is more surprised than me that Summer consented to be my date for the evening. I'm a very happy and lucky man. Now if you'll excuse us we have friends to chat with."

Their dirty looks did not go unnoticed but he pretended it didn't bother him and ushered Summer the table where his brothers sat.

He was glad that people stopped them to say hello as they walked. Many people didn't share the same opinion of those two biddies. Summer's death grip on his hand loosened and began to relax as she joined in with the jokes and laughter.

The band started playing what Luke dubbed "lovey dovey music."

Holden laughed. "I think that's my cue. Would you like to dance?" He stood and offered his hand to her.

Grasping it she smiled and her eyes shined bright. "Yes."

He led her to the dance floor and immediately drew her against him. Her shoulders were so soft. He put his hand on her back and led her around the dance floor, loving the feel of her in his arms. She had said she was falling in love with him too. His heart hoped so because she made him whole. He pulled her closer leaning his cheek against her soft hair. She smelled of vanilla and cinnamon and she was intoxicating. They danced perfectly together as if they had danced together many times before. Her gracefulness reflected in each step. Finally, the music stopped and they drew apart, staring into each other's eyes. The love she held for him shone in her eyes and he hoped she could see the same in his.

He led her back to the table and was not surprised to see Mindy Sue sitting next to Matt. They seemed to like each other and he was glad.

"Hi, Mindy Sue," Summer said.

"Hey guys. Nice moves on the dance floor," Mindy Sue enthused. "Oh, I almost forgot. Some woman named Sheila called the office all day."

Matt turned pale. Holden swore under his breath and Summer looked at him with her eyebrows raised. "Thanks for letting me know." He was going for casual but his voice sounded gruff.

Summer pushed her chair back and stood. She leaned over and whispered. "I'm going to the ladies room."

Holden nodded, his thoughts were on Sheila, wondering what she wanted.

SUMMER SEETHED INSIDE as she plastered a smile on her face and made her way through the crowd. Who was Sheila and why did Holden act like it was nothing when Matt turned so white? Something didn't add up and it felt as though a weight was on her chest. The ladies room was crowded but she just wanted to wash her hands. The cold water might make her feel better, plus she needed to step away from Holden for a few. She had no details but something wasn't right.

Trust was important to her. She'd known all along that something happened in Texas. That something just might be named Sheila, and the more she thought about it the more upset she got. Leaving the ladies' room, she battled her way through the crowd to the front door. She needed to breathe. She felt stifled. The heavy metal door shut behind her. The air was cooler than it had been all summer, and it felt wonderful. She leaned back against the wooden building and stared up at the moon, which wasn't quite full. She pushed off from the building and wandered over to a swing, brushing it off and sitting on it before she pushed off. Life had been so simple when her parents were alive. Since then it had been one thing after another. She missed her parents and she also missed Paul. Paul had been like a father to her. His murder still made her shudder.

"Hello, Summer, long time no see. Oh, I did see you. In a truck?" Brent's voice sounded evil and the expression on his face was one of triumph as he grabbed her, pulled her up from the swing and put his hand over her mouth.

She kicked and fought to get away. She bit his hand but he still managed to drag her toward his truck. No matter what she couldn't allow him to put her in it. He'd murder her for sure. Her adrenaline kicked in and she kicked him in the leg as hard as she could with her heel.

Brent yelped and loosened his grip to slap her. It was the opportunity she was waiting for. Screaming, she made a run for it. She heard him behind her, but she also saw Gabe running her way. For being as giant as a refrigerator, he ran surprisingly fast. He ran past her and tackled Brent.

Denver was right behind. Once they had him handcuffed, Denver used his cell phone and called Holden and then the police.

Relief washed over Summer but the glaring hate she saw in Brent's eyes terrified her. He'd had her fooled the whole time they dated.

Holden sprinted to her side, followed by his brothers and she was never so glad to see them all. She grabbed Holden around the neck and couldn't let go. His safe strong arms were her haven. He held her tight and rocked her until the sheriff showed up.

Sheriff Brown didn't seem to be in a great hurry as he ambled over to them. He shook his head when he saw Brent on the ground. "I thought for sure you had lit out of this area." He glanced at her. "Come on, you both are going to jail."

Summer gasped and cried out. "No, I'm not! I don't know why you hate me so much but I am not a part of his crimes. I'm a victim."

Holden stepped toward the sheriff, his hands clenched by his side. "We already know who is behind this. What I want to know is why you didn't investigate. It was easy enough to find the evidence."

"There is no evidence," the sheriff sneered

"Tell that to the investigator I hired."

Summer's eyes widened. "What evidence?"

Holden turned and gazed at her. "Paul told his brother, Andy he was going to put you in his will. The bar and grill belongs to you." He gave the sheriff a look of accusation. "The good sheriff here knew about it and somehow the lawyer never got a hold of you."

"What?" Summer put her hand over her mouth to keep the screams in. Paul died because of her. It was almost too much to take in.

"Some of the hands where Brent last worked said that Brent suddenly came into some money. They figure that's why he quit. Summer had nothing to do with it." Holden

141

grasped her hand and drew her to his side. "She's not going anywhere."

Sheriff Brown's face turned red. "You haven't proven one thing."

Colt and Caleb rounded the corner with Andy Gallagher. They held him between them, their hands wrapped tight around his arms. He was swearing up a storm.

Summer glanced up at Holden. "I don't understand."

"You will, honey."

The sheriff frowned. "You O'Malleys let him go. What do you think you're doing?"

Colt spoke up. "Let me see. How does this work? The killer usually rats out the person who paid them for a reduced sentence. Isn't that right, Caleb?"

"Happens all the time. The actual murderer gets less time than the person that planned the whole thing," Caleb answered. "Of course it depends on who confesses first."

Andy's face turned red. "I didn't pull the trigger. I'm not doing more time."

Brent was still on the ground, flanked by Denver and Gabe. "Shut the hell up!"

Sheriff Brown called for backup, then he handcuffed Andy. "Hell, Andy, why'd you have to do it? You've been a pillar here in Carlston. I'm finding it hard to believe."

Andy didn't make eye contact with anyone. It was as though he was suddenly ashamed. "She had my brother twisted around her little finger. Do you know who built that bar and grill? My father did."

Tremendous sadness and guilt filled Summer. If not for her, Paul would be alive. It was almost too much to bear. A lump formed in her throat and the back of her eyes burned. Her heart ached in a way she'd never experienced before. She watched as the deputies took the two men away. There was no thank you from the sheriff. The men began to congratulate each other and it was just too much. She burst into tears. Holden held her while she sobbed and she wrapped her arms around his waist. He rubbed her back and whispered encouraging words until finally she was too drained to cry anymore.

She let go of him, embarrassed by her outburst. "I got your shirt wet."

He bestowed her with a loving smile. "Sweetheart, it's all good. Ready to go home?"

Summer hiccupped and nodded, allowing Holden to lead her to the truck. Her limbs felt heavy and her head hurt. She couldn't stop thinking about Paul and his horrible death. The guilt overwhelmed her. She leaned her head back against the seat and closed her eyes.

CHAPTER TEN

*I*t hurt to watch Summer. She looked so devastated and Holden wished he could take her pain away. He thought that catching Brent would be cause for celebration. It was for everyone but Summer. He could read her pain in her eyes. She'd been quiet the last two days and that worried him. He sat in the kitchen drinking coffee, listening to the hum of the vacuum cleaner upstairs. The house never looked cleaner, she never stopped. She just cleaned and cleaned. She needed to keep busy but when was she going to stop?

He'd gone to her bed the last two nights and held her. She no longer cried but she seemed to need his comfort. Last night she'd had some sort of nightmare and woke up. He pulled her close and she went right back to sleep. Besides that, he felt helpless. He wished he knew what to do.

His cell phone rang. It was Sheila again and he hit ignore. He never should have allowed that woman into his life. She was pure poison and he wished he could ignore her, but sooner or later he'd have to deal with her, again.

Paul's lawyer had stopped by yesterday to tell Summer

KATHLEEN BALL

she was the sole owner of the Bar and Grill and there was a good bit of cash that Paul wanted her to have. She seemed even more distressed by the news.

Enough was enough, he went outside and saddled two of his calmer horses. When he came in the vacuum was still going. Holden marched up the steps and unplugged it.

Summer turned and stared at him. "Too loud? I can do something else."

The circles under her eyes ate at him. "No, honey, we're going for a ride."

Summer sighed. "I don't want to go into town today."

Holden stepped in front of her and gently put his hands on her shoulders. He gave her what he hoped was a sexy grin. "No town. We're going horseback riding."

She stared into his eyes and gave him a semblance of a smile.

"Good!" He took her hand, led her down the stairs and out the front door. Before she could object he had her mounted on Links while he jumped into the saddle on Jessie. They started out slow and easy. They didn't talk and she looked as though she was enjoying herself. She even smiled. The next thing he knew Summer was flying by him. He admired her riding. He gave Jessie a kick and off they went.

Summer pulled Links up at the pond. Her smile brightened her whole face. "I guess I won."

Holden laughed. "I didn't know we were racing, honey." He dismounted and went to get Summer down from Links. He made sure that her body slid against his as he lifted her down. A spark of desire flickered so quickly in her eyes he wasn't sure if it was wishful thinking or not.

Summer led Links to the water and Jessie followed. "This was a great idea. Thank you." She smiled at him again.

"I've been worried about you. Talk to me, Summer, tell me what's eating at you."

"I keep going round and round and I can't get past the part where I'm to blame for Paul's death. I even dated his killer. I try to tell myself that it's not my fault but everything inside of me screams that it is my fault."

He wanted to put his arms around her, but he wanted her to talk more.

"Paul gave me a place to live and a job. He liked Brent too and he listened to me when I was down. In fact when Brent broke it off, Paul defended Brent's reason of our schedules being too different."

"Awe, honey, obviously Brent fooled Paul too. No one that worked with him thought him capable of murder. It's not as if you missed anything."

She stared at him thoughtfully and was silent for a few minutes. "That makes sense. Why did he stick around? He must have known he'd get caught."

"From what I gathered, Andy decided not to pay him unless you were dead too, since you had witnessed it."

"What?" Summer's voice squeaked.

"Paul told Andy he was going to change the will but Paul had already done it. Somehow they had the idea that you wouldn't be there or something."

"That does make sense. Wednesday night was my night to work a shorter shift. It was busier than usual, so I stayed and helped Paul." Summer sighed and sat on the lush grass.

Holden sat beside her and pulled her down until he was on his back with her head nestled on his shoulder. "The main thing is that you are fine and they have been caught."

"You're right. I guess I feel a bit better but I still feel heartbroken about the whole thing."

Caressing her blond hair, he turned and kissed her forehead. It felt so right to be together. This is what's been missing from his life—or rather who. He wanted her so badly it hurt but he knew she was too fragile. He'd just hold her for now and hope she would stop blaming herself. Maybe today they made strides toward that.

"I'd hate to think what would have happened to me if not for you and your brothers, Holden. Oh and I can't forget your merry band of protectors." She traced the buttons on his shirt.

"I think we should head back before Luke and John decide to find us. Have you noticed they don't like you out of sight too long?" Holden kissed her forehead once more and sat up, bringing her with him.

"I noticed." Summer stood and wiped the grass off her jeans. "It's nice though, almost like I'm part of the family."

Holden had the sudden urge to wipe the grass off the back of her jeans. He quickly lifted her up and practically threw her on Links. "Honey, you are part of the family." Her smile warmed his heart.

They made good time getting back and Mark and Luke offered to take care of Jessie and Links. Hand in hand they strolled inside.

"What would you like for dinner?" She asked. She stopped suddenly and he glanced to see what she was staring at.

"Whatever you're making," Sheila answered from the kitchen in a low sultry voice.

His body stiffened and he silently cursed his fate. He gave Summer's hand a quick squeeze and let her go. The first thing he noticed was that Matt was missing from his usual place on the couch. He was relieved. "What are you doing here?"

"Visiting of course. I knew once you got settled you'd want me to join you." Her big, brown, doe eyes studied him.

He wasn't going to get lost in those eyes again. They might look like doe eyes but they actually belonged to the devil. Her long brown hair hung down her back and she wore a sexy halter top with a denim skirt. Her legs stretched forever and she filled out her top. Devil he reminded himself. "Who let you in?"

"Darling, Matt. I'm not sure if he was happy to see me or not. He certainly appeared surprised when I told him you asked me to come." She smiled at him, ignoring Summer.

He could feel Summer's eyes boring into him. He hoped she trusted him enough to know he didn't invite another woman to visit. "I didn't ask you to come. In fact, the last time you called, I asked you to stop calling."

She stepped closer to them. He'd forgotten just how tall she was.

"I'm not calling, I'm visiting. There is a big difference." Her gaze flickered to Summer and she dismissed her. "I never cancelled the wedding plans. Everything is still in place for next month."

"Where are you staying?" Summer asked, her irritation evident.

Sheila frowned. "I guess I didn't think that far ahead. I'll sleep with Holden."

Summer elbowed Holden and when he glanced down at her, her blue eyes were full of fury.

"Listen Sheila, that's not going to happen." He ran his fingers through his hair trying to figure out a way to get Sheila to leave. She had a volatile personality and anything could set her off.

Sheila folded her arms under her chest making it look bigger. "I don't see why not. We always did before."

"Not any more. I had to get a restraining order, remember?"

She laughed. "A piece of paper can't separate us." She smiled at Summer. "I'm Sheila, Holden's Fiancée."

Summer summoned up a smile and put her hand out to shake Sheila's. "Nice to meet you. If I'd known you were coming I'd have made a hotel reservation for you. As it is we're short on bedrooms. Poor Matt is sleeping on the couch."

Sheila shook Summer's hand. "Well, then I can camp out here with Matt—"

"No! You will go nowhere near my brothers. Actually, I think you should leave." His patience was wearing thin.

"Fine. You said there's a hotel in town?" She asked Summer.

Summer nodded. "It's at the far edge of Carlston. You can't miss it."

Sheila smiled at them both. "All righty then. I'll be going. See you soon," she said as she sailed out the door.

He wasn't sure what he expected from Summer but it wasn't calm silence. It surprised and worried him. She waltzed over to the kitchen and stood at the kitchen sink peering out the window. "Summer, I'm so sorry."

"I know." Now he could hear the tears in her voice.

"We are not engaged. I have a restraining order against her."

She turned and gave him a sad smile. "But you were engaged at one time. I kept wondering why you moved from Texas. I realized that it was a private matter. I assumed one of the boys got in trouble or something and you wanted a new start. A woman didn't occur to me. I mean I figured you must have dated, though I couldn't imagine when you found the time between college and taking care of your brothers." She shrugged and grabbed the coffee pot, poured out the old coffee and began to make a fresh pot. "What now?"

"I'm not putting you off but I need to get to Matt. What happened concerns him and I need to check on him."

"Well, don't explain, go. I hope Matt is okay. Bring him home when you find him."

He smiled and nodded realizing how wonderful Summer

really was. He took off and raced to the barn. Mark was there cleaning stalls. "Where's Matt?"

"Is the barracuda gone?"

"Yes, where is he?"

"He called Mindy Sue to come get him. We were all pole-axed when Sheila knocked on the door. Then she acted as though nothing happened and wanted to know if we had rented out tuxes for the wedding. You've got a big problem, Holden."

"She's nuts!" Luke called from the hat loft.

"And stupid!" yelled John.

Mark smirked. "Yeah, she kept getting Luke and John mixed up."

Holden sighed. "I'm glad y'all left the house. I need to make a few calls to see what we can do about her. Did Matt say when he'd be back?"

"When hell freezes over!" John yelled.

"He said to call when she was gone!" Luke shouted.

"Call him and tell him to ask Mindy Sue to dinner, this way Summer won't ask too many questions before I get some answers."

Mark nodded "Good idea. What did Summer say? She's not mad is she?"

Holden walked toward the barn door he turned his head. "Not yet." She would be. He was on borrowed time.

"SHEILA," Summer let the name roll off her tongue. She's never known a Sheila before. She had to admit that she was beautiful without an ounce of fat one her. Well, except for her chest. It had taken all the manners her mother had taught her to keep from going ballistic in Sheila's face. What was all this about a wedding that was still planned? Her heart sank and she felt queasy. It was one thing after another and she was tired, just so damn tired. She wasn't even sure that the whole other woman thing had hit her yet. Holden was hers now, wasn't he? Why did everything have to be so hard? Just when she thought she could get through her latest problems this came up. Maybe she and Holden weren't meant to be. Her heart cried no, but her head said maybe.

If that woman did anything to Matt. She shook her head. She loved those boys and she didn't care what happened with Holden. It was not going to impact her relationship with them, she vowed.

She'd have to wait for Holden to explain what happened. It must have been pretty bad for him to uproot his family. Her mind raced as she started dinner, baked chicken and mashed potatoes. She looked forward to mashing the potatoes. She really needed to do something to get out some of her frustrations.

By the time she was done, Mark, Luke and John walked in. Matt and Mindy Sue were next. She studied each face looking to see if they were all right. They seemed disgruntled all except for Matt who appeared madder than hell. Fortunately, Mindy Sue kept chatting at him.

They were getting ready to sit down to dinner when Holden came through the door. He had a package in one hand and flowers in the other. He put the package on the couch and made a beeline for her. They were wild flowers of all colors. Tears pricked her eyes. No one other than her father had ever given her flowers. Her hands shook as she reached out for them. Holden leaned in and kissed her lips. She prepared for a small kiss but he deepened it until the others applauded.

Turning red, she broke off the kiss but she couldn't hide her smile of pleasure. He was a special man. "Sit, you're just in time for dinner. Thank you for the flowers."

Holden winked and gave her a sexy smile. "I was hoping you'd like them."

Her cheeks grew warmer. "I do. Let's eat."

Conversation was about everything and anything except for their surprise guest. Mindy Sue's hair was multicolored, red and purple, with some of the green from the other day. On anyone else it would have looked a bit strange but Mindy Sue carried it off as usual. Her nails were purple with green tips. More than anything, Summer enjoyed the way she and Matt smiled at each other. They were a cute couple.

Luke took a big bite of mashed potatoes and proceeded to ask what was in the package, but Holden just told him not to speak with his mouth full. It was funny to watch Luke try to swallow as quickly as he could. "What's in the bag?"

"Something for y'all," Holden replied with a teasing smile.

"Please?" John asked with his puppy dog look.

Summer knew that Holden had trouble saying no to that particular expression.

"Go get it John and bring it on over," Holden instructed.

John shot out of his wooden chair and was back just as fast. He reached into the bag and brought out a new video game they'd been wanting. Then he held up an updated game console that had four controllers. "Wow!"

Matt laughed. "Maybe I'll actually get a chance to play."

"Yeah right," Mark kidded. "Who has been lying on the couch mastering game after game?"

"Thanks, Holden, now I won't have to be last anymore," Luke enthused.

Summer cocked her head to one side. "Why would you always be last?"

"Because the youngest shouldn't be last, so I am."

"Luke, that is so sweet." Summer smiled.

"No, I'm anything but sweet. Don't try to make a girl of me."

She had to bite her bottom lip to keep from laughing. "I wouldn't think of it and you are right, sweet is not the right word. How about mature? It was very mature of you to do that."

Luke smiled and gave all his brothers an "I told you so" look.

They shoveled their food into their mouths and inhaled the rest of the dinner. Before she knew it she was alone at the table with Holden. "Thank you again for the flowers. You're the first man besides my father to give me flowers. It means a lot."

Holden winked. "You mean a lot to me. This whole thing with Sheila is bound to get worse before it gets better."

Summer opened her mouth to ask why but Holden interrupted her.

"I'll tell you the whole story after my brothers are in bed. I'm worried about Matt though."

"I'll listen. You'll have to come to my room."

"It was on my list of things to do from the time I woke up this morning." He chuckled.

Summer smiled and shook her head. "You are insatiable."

"Only when you're around." His teasing smile dimmed and he grew serious. "It's true, Summer. I think I should go and watch them play video games for a while."

She stood and slowly approached him. She pulled his head against her middle and caressed his shoulder, running her fingers through his hair and kissing the top of his head. "It'll be fine."

"If we were alone, honey, I'd have you on my lap stripped naked right now."

Summer let go and laughed. "You sweet talker. Go."

Summer cleared the table and washed the dishes, glancing over at the five brothers and Mindy Sue. They were all enjoying themselves, except for Matt. His smile wasn't genuine. It didn't reach his eyes. Sheila must have done something to that sweet, young man. She went up and took her shower as usual and climbed into bed. She grabbed her latest book, western romance was her favorite, and tried to read. The book was a page turner but she couldn't concentrate. Her imagination took her places she didn't want to go.

What happened and why was Matt involved if Sheila planned to marry Holden? Nothing made sense. She didn't get a good vibe off that she devil. She was here to cause trouble and Summer realized that she would have to trust Holden to tell her the truth. Being doubted was not fun.

She had put her flowers on her nightstand earlier. They were so fragrant. Her heart filled thinking about Holden. She'd have to help him any way she could. That's what you did for the person you loved. She wasn't falling in love anymore; she'd already dove in head first.

HOLDEN WATCHED his brother's play. They were surprisingly good. He never had the time to practice and he knew his fingers and thumbs would not move as quickly as theirs did. Mindy Sue had left, kissing Matt on the cheek before going. Matt seemed a bit quiet and it worried him. This was bound to have an impact on him. Damn Sheila anyway. What was she doing in Montana?

He pictured Summer in bed all rosy from her bath and he longed to join her. Soon, he reminded himself, but he was still impatient.

Finally, he mentioned having to get up with the sun and they all agreed it was time for bed. Holden made sure that Matt was comfortable and had everything he needed. "Matt, are you okay?"

Matt nodded. "Brought back some bad memories is all. I'll

be fine. What about you? She seemed to think you're still getting hitched."

"We knew she was loco. I'll deal with her and in the meantime you can hang out with Mindy Sue."

Matt blushed. "Mindy Sue is nice."

Holden smiled. "That she is. Goodnight."

"Yep, see you in the morning."

Holden stood outside Summer's door wondering what he should say. He'd tried to move on, but it was all in front of him again. He hoped she'd listen and realize the truth of the matter. He lightly knocked and opened the door. He quickly stepped in and closed the door quietly behind him.

Summer was as rosy as he imagined. She had the flowers next to her bed and it made him glad. "You look lovely."

"Thank you. You're not so bad."

"If that's a compliment, I think you need to work on it." Holden laughed.

"Come sit next to me," she beckoned.

"I'm too riled to sit right now."

Summer nodded and peered at him expectantly.

"It's a crazy story, really. If it hadn't happened to me I'd have thought it made up." He took a deep breath and began to pace. "You already know that we lived on a ranch in Texas. I had a partial scholarship plus I applied for every grant I could find. The boys were in school, except for Matt. He declined to go to college. We couldn't afford much at that time. We had enough for our needs but it was a tough go. I went to school all day and worked the ranch until the sun went down. Homework needed to be done. Now you know why spaghetti comes out of a can."

Summer smiled encouragingly and nodded.

"Our closest neighbor was Rose Farly. She was an amazing woman. She'd lost her husband years ago but she managed her ranch and made a nice profit. She often brought desserts over for us. She sent her live in housekeeper over twice a week. I don't know what we would have done without her.

"I finally graduated and was brought into a small local practice. Things got easier. Then Rose had a stroke and her granddaughter Sheila showed up to help. We all liked her. She was fun and kind, and she began to spend a lot of time at our ranch. I figured her grandmother was better but that wasn't the case. Sheila didn't like sick people." Telling the story was harder than he thought it would be. "We became close and I thought that we were in love. My brothers' liked her and I thought why not? I asked her to marry me. It was then I went to visit Rose to get her blessing. The poor woman was half dead and the place was disgusting. I came to find out that Sheila fired the housekeeper. I had Rose rushed to the hospital and that's when all the trouble started."

"Holden, if it's too painful you don't have to tell me."

"No, you need to know. Sheila and I had our first fight and I found out she wasn't as classy as I thought. She screamed words that I never heard a woman say before. She belittled me and the ranch. She started in on my brothers. I sent them to another neighbor's place for the day. It scared me how hateful her words were and how angry she'd become. I kept waiting for her to hit me or something. She left.

"The next day she came over crying and apologizing and saying she wasn't herself. She has this way of making her eyes look so…so innocent and somehow I ended up apologizing. Rose was finally able to go back to her home and I hired a nurse. I should have trusted my instincts but I didn't. Things went back to the way they were, except she was around all the time, even when I wasn't there. She planned this grand wedding that she thought I was going to pay for. I was so foolish—I thought the down payments were the full price and I gave her the money. I noticed that none of my brothers seemed happy about the wedding. I couldn't figure it out. They loved Sheila or so I thought. Later I found out she back handed Luke and John more than once and threatened them. She had them believing that if push came to shove I'd choose her and they'd go to foster homes. She left Mark alone, I don't know why. Matt, well, Matt she did the most damage to him. She seduced him in my house. She slept with both of us. Me when I was home and Matt when I wasn't."

"Oh poor Matt."

He finally sat on the edge of the bed. "I came home early one day and caught them. I threw her out and I couldn't look at Matt. I felt that he betrayed me. Things were bad enough but they got worse. Sheila accused Matt of rape."

Summer gasped. "No way. How could she?"

"It was a huge mess. She refused to retract her statement. Matt was devastated and ashamed. It wasn't his fault. The woman is poison. To top it off she still thought we were going to get married."

"Was Matt arrested?" she asked, shocked.

"Yes and I didn't go get him right away. I'll be sorry about that decision the rest of my life. Nothing made sense and I couldn't think clearly. I forgot it takes two and when I saw them in bed, it didn't look like rape to me. The prosecutor didn't take my word for it. Matt was a minor and his name should have been kept quiet but Sheila thought it her civic duty to tell everyone about Matt."

"How long did you let Matt stay in jail?" Summer moved until she sat right next to him. She put her arms around his waist and leaned her head on his shoulder.

He appreciated her comfort. "Half a day."

"That's not so long, Holden."

"I should have been there the minute I heard about the

arrest. I bailed him out but we didn't talk. I knew he didn't rape her, but he still slept with my girl. I couldn't let the anger go at first. It started to consume me. Meanwhile Sheila still wanted to see me. I refused. She started showing up everywhere I went and I brushed her off. Finally, she cornered me and told me if I didn't let her back into my life, she was going to go through with allegations. She even threatened to hurt herself and blame it on Matt."

Summer squeezed his waist. "She's evil."

"I went to the district attorney and told him what was going on. They had me wear a wire. It was so surreal, like a movie but too much was riding on the outcome. They got their evidence. Matt was cleared and I got a restraining order."

"Why did you leave Texas?"

"Matt's name had been dragged through the mud and people still had their suspicions about him. It got ugly a couple times. I got a good price for the ranch and I figured coming up here in the middle of nowhere would suit us just fine."

"Until my problems became your problems. I'm so sorry, Holden."

He smiled and put his arms around her. "Nothing to be sorry about, honey. Last I heard she was going to be charged with some kind of false reporting or something. I didn't keep track. I really thought she was out of our lives for good."

She gazed into his eyes, her concern filled his heart. "How about you and Matt?"

"Mark almost beat me to a pulp when I wouldn't listen. Mark, Luke and John all saw how Sheila was grooming Matt to be her victim. They made me listen and now I understand that Matt was the victim of a predator. How sick is she to have sex with us both?"

Summer kissed his cheek. "And now she's here."

"Yes, now she's here." Holden sighed. "I'm going to call the authorities in Texas and see about that restraining order. I have no idea if it's a state thing or if it's good here too. Then I'll talk to Sheriff Brown and that lawyer, Rolly."

Summer snuggled closer, she felt so soft against him. "I'll help in any way I can."

His heart beat faster. "Thank you. All I need is your trust and understanding."

"You got it."

He tilted her chin up with his index finger and stared into her caring blue eyes. He leaned down and slanted his mouth over hers. She opened for him and he groaned as he deepened the kiss. His hands ran up and down her sides and rested at the sides of her breasts.

Summer trembled and kissed him back. Her hands went to his chest and then to his buttons. She made quick work of unbuttoning them as he lifted her night gown higher and higher. She lifted her bottom so he could get the gown completely up and over her head. She knocked him for a loop every time he saw her. "You're so beautiful." He leaned down and took one hard nipple into his mouth and sucked on it while his fingers tugged at the other pebbled one. Her breathing came in pants and he needed to get his jeans off. His phone rang and he almost gave into the urge to not answer it, but since an animal might need help, he pulled away and answered it.

"You naughty boy. Remember we're engaged. Don't cheat on me."

"Sheila? Where the hell are you?"

"Close enough to see you with that little skank. Get rid of her."

He heard a click and the call ended. He sat with his elbows on his knees and his face in his hands.

"I heard what she said, Holden." She quickly put her

nightgown back on. She skedaddled to the window and peered out. "I don't see anyone."

"Maybe she was guessing."

Summer closed the curtains and gave him a slight smile. "Let's hope so."

"I'd say let's go back to what we were doing but somehow she ruined the moment." Summer nodded as he stood and took her into his arms. He loved her but now wasn't the time. "We'll have our moments," he whispered. Her shiver boosted his confidence.

He let go, walked to the door and gave her a searing look before he left. Rubbing the back of his neck he went into Matt's room. Tomorrow he needed to scour the area. Sheila had been watching he just knew it. What was going on in that demented mind of hers?

CHAPTER ELEVEN

*T*he next day, Holden stared at Rolly. "What do you mean there's no restraining order?" Rolly sat behind his mahogany desk. It was surprisingly bare. A computer and a phone were the only items on it. "You had a protective order. In Texas that only lasts twenty days. You needed to go back to court to get the restraining order."

Holden slapped his Stetson against his leg. "I got bad advice then. Oh hell, now what? Can I get one here?"

"It's doubtful. She hasn't done anything here and the courts won't get involved in the mess from Texas. I wish there was more I could do."

Holden took a deep breath and sighed. "It's my own fault. I never thought she'd follow us here. That woman is out of her mind and I'm concerned."

Rolly nodded and folded his hands on his desk. "From what you've told me she could be dangerous."

"Especially since she looks and acts sane."

"Where is she staying?"

"At the hotel."

"Whatever you do, don't go there," Rolly said, leaning

forward. "She might try to pull the same crap. Don't allow anyone in your family to be alone with her."

Holden stood and leaned toward Rolly to shake his hand. "Thanks Rolly. Oh, any news about Paul's will?"

"Can't tell you. I'll pay a visit to Summer later today. Don't worry it's good news."

"We could use some good news. See you later." Holden couldn't wait to get outside. He needed fresh air. Damn Sheila; she probably knew that it was only a protective order. Damn his Texas lawyer for not telling him. He left his truck parked in front of Rolly's office and walked a half block to the clinic. He smiled at Mindy Sue and was surprised that she didn't smile back. Mindy Sue always smiled. "What's up?"

"That woman is in your office. I tried to get her to leave but she refused," Mindy Sue told him apologetically.

"It's not your fault, Mindy Sue. I guess I'd better go see what she wants." He hesitated. He wasn't in the mood to play nice and he knew if he was too mean she'd lash out in some unpredictable way. He opened the door to his office and his mouth dropped open. Sheila was laid out on his desk in a red garter belt and black stockings.

"Mindy Sue, could you come in here?" He wasn't going to let the door close. Mindy Sue walked in and froze. Her surprised gaze met his.

"What the hell are you doing lady?"

Sheila slowly got up, displaying her body for both of them to see. Holden looked away but Mindy Sue glared at her. Sheila grabbed her dress and put it on. "I don't know what all the fuss is about. I'm his fiancée and I've done this plenty of times before. Right, darling?"

"Get out." He pointed to the door.

"Well, if now isn't a good time, I'll catch you later." She gave him a sugary smile and waved to Mindy Sue before she left.

"So that's her. Matt told me the story. A real piece of work." Mindy Sue shook her head. "Next time I'll call the police."

"There'd better not be a next time." Holden frowned. Sheila was crazier than he thought. Actually she was bat shit crazy and always had been. "If she shows up again call me."

"Sure thing. I hope for all your sakes she leaves town fast. Matt's really upset. Can't say I blame him."

"Matt's not to blame for any of it. I need to head over to Stone McCoy's ranch. He took in five of the horses we found at Jacob Ash's place. I'd love to have Jacob thrown in jail but the laws aren't tough enough on animal abusers."

"I hope you find homes for them all."

"Me too. See ya later, Mindy Sue." He turned to leave and turned back. "Thanks Mindy Sue, for all you do." He left before she had a chance to reply. If Shelia had been after money he'd gladly pay her to stay away, but money wasn't her motivator. She had it in her head that she wanted him, and it creeped him out. The audacity of lying on his desk naked. The thought made him shudder. It would be too much to hope that she'd just go away.

THAT AFTERNOON, Summer pressed down on the gas pedal to her car. Damn, damn, double damn! She shouldn't have come to town but she thought with Brent behind bars things would be different. Apparently, Sheila had been in town a day before she showed up at the ranch, telling the whole town that she was Holden's fiancée. Summer's jaw hurt from grinding her teeth.

The cashier at Ander's food mart actual smirked at her and asked if she still planned to live there after the wedding. Talk about humiliation. The topper was seeing Lizzie Hoff on the sidewalk.. Lizzie sang Sheila's praises. Summer had even been treated to a wonderful story of how romantic Sheila was, with her naked surprise in Holden's office. She knew that she needed to just wipe it from her mind and talk to Holden about it later but it still stung.

She did get good news from Rolly. Apparently, Paul had considerable assets besides the Bar and Grill and he left it all to her. She was a wealthy woman now. Paul lived a very frugal existence yet he'd been rich. She'd ask Holden what he thought about selling the Bar and Grill. She wasn't sure what she wanted to do.

She just wished for once things would go her way. She wanted a life with Holden. Every time they got close something came up to keep them apart. Enough was enough. She wanted to tell him how she felt before another day went by. Too bad for Sheila. Why she thought she'd be welcomed by the O'Leary's Summer couldn't fathom. In only two days that woman had made quite the impression on the town's people. They appeared to have welcomed Sheila and frankly it hurt.

Mindy Sue's car was parked in the driveway. Summer wasn't up to a lot of questions. Hopefully Mindy Sue and Matt would have a nice visit. What Sheila did to Matt made her seethe. Turning brother against brother and crying rape. Definitely a screw loose.

Mark came out of the barn and ambled her way. "Let me help with those packages."

"Thanks, Mark, that would be great."

He stared at her and his eyebrows rose. "What's wrong?"

"Nothing, I guess I thought when the truth about Brent and the murder came out people would be nicer to me."

He gave her a sympathetic smile. "Give it time. It's still new to them."

Summer pasted on one of her smiles. "You're right. Better get this food in the house." As soon as he left, she took a deep breath, mentally shaking herself to get it together. The boys had been through enough and they didn't need to see her melt down. It took more than one deep breath but finally she felt calm. Grabbing a bag of groceries she headed for the house.

Mark was on his way out to get the rest and Mindy Sue was at his side. She waved at Summer and got into her car.

Summer walked into the house and was Matt sitting on the couch appearing dejected. "Matt, is something wrong?"

"No. Yes. I don't know. Mindy Sue's acting a bit strange toward me. I think that she can't stomach the truth about me and Sheila. I don't blame her. She told me it wasn't my fault, yet she made excuses for not staying."

She put the food on the counter and returned to Matt. Sitting next to him she put her hand on his arm. "It's not you, Matt. Apparently Sheila showed up at the clinic and made a big scene. Mindy Sue might be trying to keep it quiet. The truth is. It's all over town and Sheila has people believing she is so romantic."

"What happened?" He sounded frantic.

"I don't know the whole story. That's for Holden to tell you. Mindy Sue's not like that. She wouldn't judge you. I saw the way she looked at you even after she knew about Texas. Give her a break. I bet she thinks she's protecting your brother."

Matt ginned until his dimples appeared. "You think?"

Summer stood and started into the kitchen. "I know."

Hopefully, Matt felt a bit better. Damn Sheila and her shenanigans. It was one thing to mess with her, but messing with the O'Leary boys was asking for trouble. Poor Holden he had enough going on and he didn't need a naked Sheila. No wonder Mindy Sue acted funny. She probably didn't want to spill the beans. Mark came back in with the last of the packages. He seemed troubled too.

"Mark, what ever happened to Sheila's grandmother?"

He shrugged his shoulders. His shoulders had broadened in the little time she'd known him. "Rose? I have no idea. Why?"

"I was just wondering. Since Sheila is here, who is looking after Rose?"

"She's a nice lady, I hope she's okay. Well, back to the horses. Luke and John are practicing to be horse whisperers. The thing is that they are actually going from stall to stall whispering to the horses. Funniest thing I ever saw." He laughed.

"You're not going to tell them?"

"No, you only get to be a kid once."

"You are a very wise man, Mark."

He blushed and quickly went on his way. He was wise beyond his years. Maybe because he had to grow up so fast. School would be starting in a few weeks. Where did the summer go? Back to school shopping was needed. Those boys grew like weeds. At least they were well nurtured weeds.

Holden raced into the house. His hair looked as though he'd run his fingers through it the whole ride home. "You've been to town."

"Yes, I have. It was a very interesting visit to say the least."

"She was already naked before I entered my office. I was never alone with her. Mindy Sue was with me."

"Hold on, cowboy. I believe you."

His eyes widened. "You do? Lizzie Hoff repeated what she told you. Oh, good God. You really believe me?"

She wouldn't have been able to stop the genuine smile that spread across her face. His astonishment stuck her as funny. "Of course I believe you. Maybe you could tell Matt why Mindy Sue is reluctant to talk to him."

He leaned in and gave her a quick kiss on the lips.

"Thanks for the heads up. Mindy Sue must be trying to keep it a secret."

Her heart lightened considerably as she watched the two brothers talking. No more poor me, now everything had to be for the boys. She and Holden would be just fine. Matt, Mark, Luke and John needed her attention now. She loved them all. She finally got the analogy of the she-bear and her cubs. She felt it soul deep, the need to protect them.

Matt grabbed the phone and made a call. Holden came and stood next to her and the heat of his body did things to her insides. Hopefully, tonight they'd get a chance for some privacy.

"What are you smiling about?" he asked drawing her into the circle of his arms.

"You."

"What about me?"

She glanced at Matt to be sure that he couldn't hear them. "I was thinking about you and how well you use it."

His eyes twinkled with amusement. "What would "it" be?"

She stepped closer until their bodies met. Slowly she ground her pelvis against his. "I can feel "it"." She wanted to burst out laughing.

"It will have to see you later. Do you know what you do to me?"

She glanced down at his jeans and couldn't contain her laughter any longer. "You can't hide what I do to you."

He stepped away. "Well you can have fun later. I heard rumor that Luke and John are whispering into the horse's ears. I can only hope they aren't swear words."

"Really?"

Holden laughed. "That's what I did at their age." He winked at her before he left.

He had a way of making her feel special. She glanced at Matt who had hung up the phone. He had a smile on his face.

She had no need to ask him if things went well. She'd make extra for dinner since she had a feeling Mindy Sue would be joining them.

She put a huge pork roast in the oven. Looking around the kitchen she realized that this had become her home. The phone rang and Matt answered it.

"It's for you."

Surprised she picked up the extension in the kitchen. "Hello?"

"Dear, it's Beverly. I thought since your mother is gone and all you have no one to counsel you, I feel it my duty to help where I can. I just had a delightful lunch with Holden's fiancée, Sheila. She very distressed that you live in the house alone with Holden."

"Thanks for being such a pillar of society, Bev. I loved how you helped me with my troubles in the past. I'm going to take a pass on your advice."

"Well—"

Summer hung up. She could feel Matt's gaze upon her. She tried to appear normal, whatever that was. She really didn't know anymore. One minute she was flying high with love in her heart and the next she wanted to kick someone. "Are you okay?" Matt asked.

"I don't know. I don't think Beverly will be inviting me to tea anytime soon."

Matt laughed. "That's a good thing."

She nodded in agreement.

It never failed, his phone always rang around dinner time. Jonas asked him to stop by. Damn and the roast smelled really good. Matt and Mindy Sue were smiling at each other.

He hoped when he was done, he and Summer would be smiling like that too.

Jonas' place wasn't very far away. He mostly had cattle on his ranch. He said something about barbed wire around a cow's neck. Holden had dealt with barbed wire before, and it was never pretty.

The barn lights weren't on and he found that to be puzzling. He headed over to the house and knocked on the door. Jonas yelled for him to come in. Holden stepped into the hallway and walked toward the well-lit kitchen. His heart beat faster when he saw Sheila standing behind Jonas holding what appeared to be a gun to the back of his head. "What the hell?"

"I'm sorry but you wouldn't give me the time of day. This is your fault. If this gun accidentally goes off, you can blame yourself."

Jonas sat silently but he kept glancing from Holden to the top of the refrigerator, over and over. Holden glanced up and saw the pistol on the top of the fridge. "Well, what did you want to talk about?" He crossed his arms in front of him and leaned against the refrigerator trying to appear casual and unafraid.

"I want to talk about the wedding and I want that woman out of our house." Her eyes were so wide and glassy that Holden thought she might be on drugs. Jonas began to cough and he leaned forward, distracting Sheila enough for Holden to grab the gun and put it in his waistband behind him.

"Don't try any tricks," she warned Jonas.

"No, ma'am. I never try anything with a Taser at my head."

"It could still kill you so shut up."

Where did she get a Taser? She probably didn't know how to work it. "When did you learn to shoot?"

"None of your business. Now are we getting married or not?"

"Of course we are," Holden answered.

"Then why did you send me away from your office today?"

"Awe, sugar, it wasn't the place or time. I didn't want anyone to get the wrong impression of you."

She smiled. "Really?"

"Really."

Jonas stood up. "Well if you two love birds want to be alone."

"If you don't mind Jonas, I'll be taking Sheila here with me."

Sheila dropped her arm to her side and began to step toward Holden. Jonas came up behind her, put her in a choke hold and grabbed the Taser. As soon as he had the Taser he let go of her throat.

"Give that back!"

"I don't think so. Holden give me my gun. This little lady needs to stay put."

Holden handed Jonas his gun. Sheila made a break for it but Holden caught her, and sat her down in the chair Jonas had been sitting on. "What are you doing, Holden?"

"Not marrying you for starters."

"You promised," she shrieked.

"Well, with threats of guns, a guy will pretty much say anything the criminal wants to hear." He pulled his phone out of his pocket and dialed the sheriff's office. After speaking to one of the deputies, he put the phone down. "It seems that you're a wanted fugitive."

Sheila shook her head vehemently. "That was all a mistake. That other boy came on to me."

Holden looked at Jonas. "She's wanted for statutory rape."

Jonas frowned. "What the hell is wrong with you lady? You disgust me."

"Let the police take me. I'll just be back. Texas won't want to come and get me. I'm way too far away."

Finally, Sheriff Brown arrived with two deputies. They handcuffed a screaming Sheila and the deputies took her away.

"She's also wanted on suspicion of a murder," Sheriff Brown informed them.

Holden closed his eyes for a moment. "She killed the other kid?"

Sheriff Brown nodded. "Guess she didn't want him to testify against her."

Jonas and Holden exchanges surprised glances. "I never figured she was that dangerous." Holden admitted.

Jonas shook his head. "I just thought she was a bit loony. Wonder why she had a Taser and not a gun?"

"Background check would be my guess," the sheriff commented.

Holden nodded. "Makes sense."

"I thought the gun was real until she put it against my skull," Jonas explained. "I'd have taken her down earlier if I had known."

"She's in custody now That's all that matters." Sheriff Brown shook both men's hands and left.

Jonas grabbed a bottle and two glasses. "Whiskey?"

Holden nodded. "I need one. I never saw that coming. Not in a million years. Crazy yes, but killing?"

"I'm sorry I called you out here but I honestly thought she had a gun. She stood behind me the whole time. Guess I'm a bit rusty. I'm Army, retired."

"Not rusty at all. I appreciate all your help. I take it no cow is wrapped in barbed wire?"

They both drank down their whiskey. Jonas shook his head and reached out and shook Holden's hand.

"Well, I better get home. I have some explaining and some courting to do."

Jonas gave him a sad smile and he wondered about it all the way home.

CHAPTER TWELVE

*B*ack at the house, Summer paced back and forth in her bedroom. Decisions needed to be made and she didn't know if she had the heart to do what was right. Sheila had everyone feeling a bit anxious. How could that woman have toyed with Matt? Holden was old enough to take the hit but Matt was a different story. All the boys had been affected. Smiles and laughter weren't readily given these last few days. What they really needed was some alone time. They needed to bond and find their center. She wasn't included in the equation. They'd be better off with an older motherly type woman. She was just a distraction to Holden and he needed to concentrate on his family.

There really wasn't a reason that she couldn't just up and leave. She had money and she had a bar and grill with two apartments upstairs. Selling it would probably be the most prudent thing. All along she wanted to leave Carlston and never look back. Now she had her chance.

What to do about her breaking heart? Time was supposed to help but the love she felt for the O'Leary's was a love that ran deep. He must have loved Sheila very much, to propose to her and the whole situation must have been devastating.

"Ouch." She stubbed her toe on the leg of the bed. She went to the window and peered outside wondering if Sheila was spying on her. Let her, she'd just see Summer in her nightgown, pacing back and forth.

No wonder the boys weren't thrilled when she first came, looking for work. They probably thought she'd fall in love with Holden, and be another Sheila. They were right about one thing. She loved him heart and soul. She'd never loved so deeply or completely but her needs were not a priority now.

Her toe throbbed as she walked back and forth. She saw the headlights before she heard the truck pull up. Her room was dark and she hoped that she didn't have to deal with Holden tonight. Her mind was overloaded. Her thinking seemed circular to her and she was right back to where she started. She continued to pace.

The soft knock on her door set her heart racing. Hesitating, she debated whether or not to open it. Holden walked in anyway. He turned on the light and immediately searched her out. He took two long strides and scooped her up into his powerful arms.

"What are you doing?" she squeaked.

"I need you. I need you to hold me." The sadness in his eyes grabbed at her heart.

"Of course. Let's lay down and I'll hold you all you want."

Holden set her on the bed and took his boots off. The weariness creased on his face worried her. Summer lay down and opened her arms to him and he immediately got into bed and wrapped his arms around her. They lay on their sides facing each other, Summer rubbed his tense back. "Were you able to save the cow?"

He pulled her closer and lay on his back putting her head on his shoulder. "There wasn't a cow."

Summer lifted her head and stared at him. "What happened?"

Holden took a deep breath and sighed. "Sheila had what we thought was a gun to Jonas' head."

"Oh no! Is Jonas all right? What did she want?"

He closed his eyes for a moment as though he was gathering his thoughts. "Jonas is fine. She wanted me to marry her."

"What? How did all this happen?"

"Somehow she got the drop on Jonas and made him call me. I walked into the kitchen and Sheila had a gun pointed at the back of Jonas' head. Came to find out it was a Taser."

Summer gasped. "Still, that could have killed him."

"Jonas motioned to me with his eyes where his gun was. He distracted her, I grabbed the gun and then Jonas grabbed Shelia and got the Taser from her."

"What is wrong with her? She could have gotten you two killed. Where is she now?"

Holden smiled. "It's fine, she's in jail. She's wanted in Texas for murder."

Tears trailed down her face. "Murder? How? Oh God, I'm so glad that you're okay."

Holden wiped away a tear from her face with his thumb. "Yes I do know. He's kicking himself for letting Sheila get the upper hand. And yes, murder. There was another boy after Matt she raped then killed."

"Oh no, she is pure evil. Hopefully, Jonas will get over it. He's such a nice man He's a retired soldier you know." She hugged him tighter.

" Yes I do know. Is he nicer than me?"

She laid her head on his chest before answering. It was all too hard. Of course Holden was nicer but it wouldn't be right to lead him on. Her future lay elsewhere. The family needed time alone to heal and she wasn't part of the family. Her stomach clenched as a lump formed in her throat. She didn't know what to say, so she said nothing. Remembering the feel of his arms around her, and the way he smelled of soap and leather was imperative. She needed to remember so she'd have something to hold on to when she left.

She wished she was brave enough to tell him of her decision. She had enough money saved to take her pretty far and she'd talk to Rolly about listing the Bar and Grill for sale. The rest of her inheritance would be deposited in her account within the month. Holden's strong hands rubbed her back. Little did he know he was comforting her for the decision she'd made to leave. Her body ached to make love to him one more time, but it wouldn't be fair to him. Finally, she felt him relax and his breathing became even. It took everything inside her to leave the comfort of his embrace. She choked back a sob and covered her mouth with her hand. Quickly and quietly, she packed a few of her belongings. She could buy new things later, she couldn't take a chance on Holden waking up.

Taking on last look at him was a mistake. He looked so serene and his hair fell over his brow enticing her to brush it back, but she resisted the urge. She tiptoed out of the room and down the stairs.

"Leaving?" Matt asked.

Summer's heart sank. "Yes. I'm so sorry."

"It's fine, Summer. Everything around here has been pretty messed up lately."

"No, it's not fine but it's for the best. You and your brothers need to heal."

Matt nodded. "Does Holden know?"

"No, I'm taking the coward's way out. I want you to have a new beginning."

"I'm going to miss you. Come back when you figure out that your new beginning is here with us."

Tears poured down her face as she nodded. There was nothing left to say. She slowly opened the front door and quietly closed it behind her. Her life was in pieces and she wasn't sure how'd she go on from here but she didn't have a choice. She got into her car and drove away.

WAKING WITH THE SUN, Holden hopped out of bed. It was nice to wake up in Summer's bed. He planned to propose to her and they'd wake up together every morning. She was his heart and it was time that she knew it. Now that their problems were behind them, they could work on their relationship.

He was surprised to see Matt sitting at the kitchen table looking as though he lost his best friend. He hoped it wasn't something to do with Mindy Sue. He'd hoped that they would be happy together. Young love could be fickle.

Holden pulled back one of the kitchen chairs and sat across from Matt. "Woman problems?"

Matt's eyes were bloodshot as though he hadn't slept. "You could say that. Holden, Summer left last night."

He felt gut kicked and it suddenly became hard to breath. "What are you talking about?"

Matt shook his head morosely. "She said we needed to heal and she wanted us to have a new beginning."

"Anything else?"

"Yeah, she was crying something awful. I don't think she wanted to leave."

Holden ran his fingers through his hair. Was it all women or only the ones he got mixed up with? Damn, he never should have trusted her to stay. "I'll go over to Caleb's and talk to her."

"I don't think she's there. I think she left town." Matt's eyes grew moist.

"Well, that's that. I guess I better make some coffee and then breakfast." Holden tried to act as though his heart wasn't breaking. He had too much to do and his brothers were going to be upset.

How he got through the day, he'd never know. Mark didn't say much, he just spent his day in the barn. Luke was pissed as hell and he kept muttering about liars. John cried and Holden wished he could have cried with him. That wasn't an option. He was their rock and he had to be strong. The house seemed empty without her. He expected to see her at every turn. Loneliness pumped through his veins.

Finally, everyone went to bed. Holden sat on the front porch in the dark. Her betrayal was too much to bare. As he remembered their last moments together he wondered if she had already planned to leave. How long ago had she made the decision? A complete ass is what he was. He'd been planning a life together and she'd been planning her escape. It hurt bone deep and he was at a loss as to how to deal with his pain. Peering up into the night sky, he wondered how they would get through the next few days.

———

HOLDEN WAS WEARY. It had been almost a week since Summer had left and things hadn't gotten any easier. He worried about her. A for sale sign now hung in the front window of the bar and grill. Somehow that made the whole situation real for him. On top of that Mrs. Ruth refused to take Mrs. Grady's chickens. It had something to do with someone winning first prize with a pie. All he knew was that he had to take the chickens out to Stone McCoy's place. He had an empty chicken coop.

It wasn't a long drive to Stone's place, and when he arrived, Stone was outside waiting for him.

"I wouldn't worry, Holden," Stone told him as he helped put the chickens in his coop. "These biddies will want their chickens back in a day or two. By the way when are you going after your woman?"

"She left, end of story."

"Oh hell, Holden, sometimes you have to go after the prize and from what I know of Summer she is the best prize for you. Have you seen how that little gal looks at you? She loves you, swallow your damn cowboy pride and go get her."

Holden shrugged his shoulders "If she wanted me she would have stayed.

"Well, I heard she left to give you a new beginning and she was crying when she left."

Holden gave Stone a hard glare. "Who'd you hear that from?"

Stone grinned. "Your brother, Matt. I called to see how you were. I can only tell you that I have a past love that I'd give anything to be able to find. You just have to drive to the next town. Cherry Street I believe, the house with the blue shutters."

"You know something Stone, you're a real pain in the ass. Thanks, I have a drive to make." Holden jumped into the driver's seat of his truck and gunned the engine. He was headed for Cherry Street.

SUMMER GLANCED around her rented house and sighed. There was one nice thing about living in a new town, no one knew her. The one bad thing about living in a new town was the loneliness. She'd been waiting for the air conditioner technician to come. The heat was brutal and no matter what she did, she couldn't stop perspiring. Any other day, she'd go and sit in a cool café, instead of sweltering. Good thing it was a month to month lease, she couldn't imagine staying here permanently. Once she received the money for her inheritance she'd be able to afford something much nicer. She'd been looking for a job, applying everywhere she could. She thought that the bartending job would probably come through. It wasn't easy without references. Paul was dead and she didn't want anyone to call the O'Leary's place. She needed a clean break from them. They were ever on her mind, especially Holden. He most likely hated her now for sneaking away in the night. He wouldn't understand, hell, she wasn't sure she understood the whole thing. Summer longed to go back but she refused to be a detriment to those boys.

She wondered if Holden had taken them to get back to school clothes or if Matt had his cast off yet. She still had nightmares and checked and rechecked the doors and windows at night. Pouring herself a glass of iced tea she put the cold glass against her forehead hoping it would cool her. She heard a truck pull up and put the glass on the counter and hurried to the door. She quickly opened it and was stunned to see Holden.

Her heart squeezed painfully. "What? How? You're here."

He stared at her as though he was trying to memorize her face. His Adam's apple bobbed up and down. "Stone knew where you were staying." He continued to stare.

His black hair was longer, and he had circles under his eyes. He seemed suddenly hesitant as though he realized he made a mistake in coming. She half expected him to turn and leave. Tears formed in her eyes as she realized just how much she loved him. Holden leaned down and put his lips against hers. He kissed his way to her heart. "Don't cry, it breaks my heart to see you cry."

Summer pulled back. "It does? It breaks your heart?"

He drew her into a bear hug and rocked her back and forth for a minute. "I love you."

"I'm no good for you. But you love me? Really?" Summer pulled back to see his eyes. They were filled with love, real love. Tears poured down her face faster. "I didn't think, I didn't know…"

"I never told you and I should have. I thought you knew how I felt and I prayed that you felt the same."

Summer nodded her head. "I do love you and that's why I left. I'm no good for your family. As soon as the boys go to school, they'll be outcasts because of me. I couldn't bear that."

"Honey, there are only two people in town that might still have something to say about you, but they have something to say about everyone in the town. Nothing has been right since you left, hell Mrs. Grandy and Mrs. Ruth won't share the chickens, Yukon has been moping. Luke thinks it's his fault and John is lost without you."

"I don't know, Holden."

"Why is it so damn hot in here?"

"The air doesn't work."

"Summer please grab your things. I want you home with me. I can't sleep at night worrying about you, missing you. Honey, I love you so damn much." He put his hands on the sides of her face, framing it. "I wouldn't care if the whole town was talking about you. I'm empty without you."

She bit her lip wondering what to do.

"Summer, I want us to have a life together. I know it's asking a lot with my four brothers and all but I want you to be my wife. I want—"

"Yes! I love you too. I have for a very long time. I thought I was doing you a favor by leaving, but I just made both of us miserable. I love your brothers and you once said that you were a package deal. I happen to love the whole package."

"Excuse me, I hate to interrupt and all but do you still

want the air fixed?" They had been so lost in each other, they didn't notice the repairman.

"Hell, yes. I'd hate for the next tenant to swelter to death. I'll show you where it is."

The repairman laughed. "I already know, this isn't the first time I've had to repair that old thing and it probably won't be the last."

Summer turned to Holden. "I can be packed in no time. I seem to travel light." She started toward the bedroom. "What about my car? Should I follow you?"

"No, honey. I want you with me. I'll send someone to come pick it up."

His answer ignited her heart.

EPILOGUE

*S*ummer and Holden stood arm in arm watching the beautiful Montana sunset. It was the end of summer and fall would be coming soon. Holden had proposed again, this time with a beautiful diamond ring. Summer's heart melted every time she looked at it. She breathed in the clean air and smiled. Coming back had been the right choice for everyone. Matt finally got his cast removed and became a real leader to his brothers, teaching them about training horses.

"So, Mrs. Grandy has the chickens now?" she asked, then chuckled. "It took a while for them to get over their fight."

"You don't mess with someone's prize winning pie recipe nor do you borrow it. Stone was glad to see the chickens gone. Rolly called; he found a buyer for your bar and grill. Some woman named Autumn bought it."

Summer smiled. "Good, one less thing to worry about. So, my sweet cowboy, do we set the date?"

"I put a call into a clinic in Great Falls. As soon as they have someone who can cover for me we'll set the date. I have a feeling if I don't get a temporary replacement I'll be called out in the middle of the ceremony."

"You know what? The day I answered your ad for a nanny position was the luckiest day of my life. There were nights that I thought I'd break, wanting to be back here with you."

Holden took her into his arms and kissed her deep and hard. "You'll have the rest of your life to make it up to me."

She shook her head at the teasing look in his eyes. "I'd be glad to if we could just find some privacy."

ABOUT THE AUTHOR

Sexy Cowboys and the Women Who Love Them...
Finalist in the 2012 and 2015 RONE Awards.
Top Pick, Five Star Series from the Romance Review.
Kathleen Ball writes contemporary and historical western romance with great emotion and
memorable characters. Her books are award winners and have appeared on best sellers lists including: Amazon's Best Seller's List, All Romance Ebooks, Bookstrand, Desert Breeze Publishing and Secret Cravings Publishing Best Sellers list. She is the recipient of eight Editor's Choice Awards, and The Readers' Choice Award for Ryelee's Cowboy.
Winner of the Lear diamond award Best Historical Novel-
Cinders' Bride
There's something about a cowboy

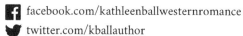

facebook.com/kathleenballwesternromance

twitter.com/kballauthor

instagram.com/author_kathleenball

So Many Roads to Choose

The Settlers

Greg

Juan

Scarlett

Mail Order Brides of Spring Water

Tattered Hearts

Shattered Trust

Glory's Groom

Battered Soul

Romance on the Oregon Trail

Cora's Courage

Luella's Longing

Dawn's Destiny

Terra's Trial

Candle Glow and Mistletoe

The Kabvanagh Brothers

Teagan: Cowboy Strong

Quinn: Cowboy Risk

Brogan: Cowboy Pride

Sullivan: Cowboy Protector

Donnell: Cowboy Scrutiny

Murphy: Cowboy Deceived

Fitzpatrick: Cowboy Reluctant

Angus: Cowboy Bewildered

Rafferty: Cowboy Trail Boss

Shea: Cowboy Chance

The Greatest Gift
Love So Deep
Luke's Fate
Whispered Love
Love Before Midnight
I'm Forever Yours
Finn's Fortune
Glory's Groom

Made in United States
North Haven, CT
09 April 2022

18061471R10108